DALMATIAN PRESS

# *American*
# CLASSICS
# FOR CHILDREN
### COLLECTION II

# *American* CLASSICS FOR CHILDREN

## COLLECTION II

### *Little Women*

LOUISA MAY ALCOTT

·:· ⇥〣⇤ ·:·

### *Pollyanna*

ELEANOR H. PORTER

·:· ⇥〣⇤ ·:·

### *Rebecca of Sunnybrook Farm*

KATE DOUGLAS WIGGIN

Dalmatian ❧ Press

The Dalmatian Press American Classics for Children
have been adapted and illustrated with care and thought,
to introduce you to a world of famous authors, characters, ideas,
and great stories that have been loved for generations.

Editor — Kathryn Knight
Creative Director — Gina Rhodes
And the entire classics project team of Dalmatian Press

ALL ART AND ADAPTED TEXT © DALMATIAN PRESS, LLC

ISBN: 1-40370-472-4

First Published in the United States in 2003 by Dalmatian Press, LLC, USA

Copyright © 2003 Dalmatian Press, LLC

Printed and bound in the U.S.A.

The DALMATIAN PRESS name and logo are
trademarks of Dalmatian Press, LLC, Franklin, Tennessee 37067.

12598

03  04  05  06  07  LBM  15  14  13  12  11  10  9  8  7  6  5  4  3  2  1

# FOREWORD

*A note to the reader—*

Three American classic stories rest in your hands. The characters are famous. The tales are timeless.

Each story has been carefully condensed and adapted from the original version (which you really *must* read when you're ready for every detail). We kept the well-known phrases for you. We kept the author's style. And we kept the important imagery and heart of each tale.

Literature is terrific fun! It encourages you to think. It helps you dream. It is full of heroes and villains, suspense and humor, adventure and wonder, and new ideas. It introduces you to writers who reach out across time to say: "Do you want to hear a story I wrote?"

Curl up and enjoy.

# DALMATIAN PRESS
# AMERICAN CLASSICS FOR CHILDREN

## COLLECTION I

*The Adventures of Tom Sawyer*
*The Adventures of Huckleberry Finn*
*Moby Dick*

## COLLECTION II

*Little Women*
*Pollyanna*
*Rebecca of Sunnybrook Farm*

# CONTENTS

LITTLE WOMEN ........................................1

ABOUT LOUISA MAY ALCOTT ......................187

POLLYANNA ..........................................189

ABOUT ELEANOR H. PORTER .....................377

REBECCA OF SUNNYBROOK FARM ...........379

ABOUT KATE DOUGLAS WIGGIN ...............565

# Little Women

LOUISA MAY ALCOTT

CONDENSED AND ADAPTED BY
BETHANY SNYDER

ILLUSTRATED BY
MARTIN HARGREAVES

# CONTENTS

Characters.................................................... 4

1. Marmee's Girls.................................... 9

2. Merry Christmas ................................ 23

3. The Laurence Boy ............................... 31

4. Burdens and Blessings ...................... 39

5. Being Neighborly .............................. 47

6. Beth's Piano Lesson .......................... 57

7. Amy Learns a Sour Lesson................. 63

8. Jo Finds Some Weak Spots ............... 69

9. Meg Has a Beauty Lesson ................. 79

10. Spring Ends – And Play Begins........ 91

11. A Summer Picnic.............................. 101

12. Castles in the Air.............................. 113

13. Autumn Secrets ............................... 121

14. The Telegram ................................... 131

15. A Bitter Winter Wind ...................... 141

16. Dark Days ........................................ 149

17. A Mother's Touch ............................ 159

18. Father's Little Women ..................... 167

19. The Year Closes................................ 175

About the Author................................ 187

THE March Family

MEG — (Margaret) 16, very pretty and sensible—with dreams of living in fine style

JO — (Josephine) 15, very tall, thin, and headstrong—with a talent for writing

BETH — (Elizabeth) 13, sweet, caring, and musically talented—but timid and shy

AMY — 12, a bit selfish, though well-mannered and ladylike—with artistic talents

MARMEE — Mrs. March, a helpful, cheery woman—the most splendid mother in the world

FATHER — Mr. March, who is off at war, serving as a chaplain

HANNAH — the family housekeeper

THE HUMMELS — a poor family with a sick newborn baby

THE KINGS — the family that Meg works for as a governess

AUNT MARCH — the grumpy old great-aunt who employs Jo to keep her company

LAURIE LAURENCE — 16, the spirited boy who lives next door to the Marches

MR. LAURENCE — Laurie's grandfather, the old gentleman next door

MR. JOHN BROOKE — Laurie's tutor, who casts his handsome brown eyes on Meg

ANNIE, BELLE, AND NED MOFFAT — Meg's friends

SALLIE GARDINER — Meg's friend

KATE, FRED, FRANK, AND GRACE — Laurie's friends from England

# Little Women

# CHAPTER ONE

## *Marmee's Girls*

"Christmas won't be Christmas without any presents," grumbled Jo, lying on the rug.

"It's so dreadful to be poor!" sighed Meg, looking down at her old dress.

"It's not fair. Some girls have plenty of pretty things, and others have nothing at all," added little Amy with a sniff.

"We've got Father and Mother, and each other," said Beth happily from her corner.

The four young faces brightened in the firelight. Then Jo said sadly, "We *haven't* got Father, and won't for a long time." The four were silent, thinking of Father far away where the fighting was.

They missed him, but they were proud of their father. He was too old to be a soldier, but he was serving as a chaplain in the war between the states.

Meg said, "Mother thinks we shouldn't spend money on Christmas presents when our men are suffering in the army. But I am afraid I don't like the idea." Meg shook her head as she thought of all the pretty things she wanted.

"We only have a dollar each to spend," said Jo. "Surely the army won't miss that. I so wanted to buy a new book."

"I planned to spend mine on new sheet music," said Beth with a little sigh.

"I shall get a box of drawing pencils," said Amy.

"Let's each buy what we want, and have a little fun. We work hard enough to earn it," cried Jo.

"I know *I* do—teaching those King children nearly all day," complained Meg.

"How would you like to care for a grumpy old lady like Aunt March all the time?" asked Jo.

"I think washing dishes and keeping things tidy is the worst work in the world." Beth looked at her rough hands with a sigh.

"At least you don't have to go to school with rude girls who laugh at your dresses," cried Amy.

"Don't you wish we had the money Papa lost when we were little, Jo?" asked Meg, who could remember better times.

"You said the other day you thought we were happier than the King children. You said they fight all the time, in spite of their money," said Beth.

"So I did, Beth. Even though we *do* have to work, we are a pretty jolly set."

Jo got up from the rug, put her hands in her pockets, and began to whistle.

"Don't, Jo. It's so boyish," said Amy.

"You should remember that you are a young lady, Jo," added Meg. "Now that you are fifteen and you wear your hair up…"

"If putting up my hair makes me a lady, I'll wear it in two tails till I'm twenty," cried Jo. "I hate to think I've got to grow up, and wear long gowns, and look nice!"

"As for you, Amy," continued Meg, "you are too critical. You'll grow up a snobby little goose, if you don't take care."

"If Jo is a tomboy and Amy a goose, what am I, please?" asked Beth.

"You're a dear," answered Meg warmly. No one disagreed, for Beth was the pet of the family.

For you, dear reader, we will take this moment to give a little sketch of the four sisters.

Margaret, the oldest, was sixteen, and very pretty. She was plump and fair, with large eyes, soft brown hair, a sweet mouth, and white hands, of which she was rather proud.

Fifteen-year-old Jo was very tall, thin, and tan. She had a strong mouth and sharp gray eyes. Her long, thick hair was her one beauty, but it was usually bundled into a net, to be out of her way.

Beth was a rosy, bright-eyed girl of thirteen. She had a shy manner, a soft voice, and a peaceful expression. She seemed to live in a happy world of her own, only going out to meet the few people whom she trusted and loved.

Amy, the youngest, was a most important person— in her own opinion at least. She had blue eyes and curling yellow hair. She was pale and slender, and was always mindful of her manners.

The clock struck six. Beth put a pair of slippers down to warm by the fire. Mother was coming, and everyone brightened to welcome her. Meg lit the lamp, and Amy got out of the easy chair without being asked. Jo held the slippers closer to the fire and said, "These are quite worn out. Marmee should have a new pair."

"I know!" said Beth. "Let's each get Marmee a Christmas gift, and not get anything for ourselves."

Meg looked at her own pretty hands. "I shall give her a nice pair of gloves."

"Army shoes," cried Jo.

"Some handkerchiefs," said Beth.

"I'll get a little bottle of perfume. I may even have some left to buy my pencils," added Amy.

"Let Marmee *think* we are getting things for ourselves, and then surprise her," said Jo. "We'll do our secret shopping tomorrow afternoon."

All four girls hooted with delight at the idea.

"Glad to find you so merry, my girls," said a cheery voice at the door. They all turned to welcome a tall, motherly lady. She was not elegantly dressed, but the girls thought the gray cloak and simple bonnet covered the most splendid mother in the world.

Mrs. March got her wet things off and her warm slippers on. Sitting down in the easy chair, she drew Amy to her lap. Meg arranged the tea table, and Jo brought wood and set chairs. Beth trotted between the parlor and the kitchen, while Amy gave directions to everyone.

After dinner, Mrs. March said, "I've got a treat for you. It's a nice long letter from Father. He sends loving wishes for Christmas, and a special message to you girls." She patted her pocket as if she had a treasure there.

"When will he come home, Marmee?" asked Beth with a little quiver in her voice.

"Not for many months, dear. He will stay as long as he can. Now come and hear the letter."

It was a cheerful, hopeful letter, full of lively descriptions of camp life, marches, and military news. At the end, Father sent a special message to his little girls at home.

"Give them all of my love and a kiss. Tell them I think of them by day and pray for them by night. I know they will be loving children to you, and do their duty faithfully. And when I come back to them I may be prouder than ever of my little women."

Everybody sniffed at that part. Amy hid her face on her mother's shoulder and sobbed, "I *am* a selfish girl! But I'll truly try to be better."

"We all will!" cried Meg. "I think too much of my looks and hate to work, but won't any more, if I can help it."

"I'll try not to be rough and wild. I'll do my duty here instead of wanting to be somewhere else," said Jo.

Beth said nothing. She wiped away her tears and began to knit a blue army sock with all her might. She resolved in her quiet little soul to be all that Father hoped for when he came home.

Mrs. March said, "We have many burdens on our road to happiness. Our longing for goodness and happiness helps us through troubles and mistakes. Now, my dears, suppose you see how far on the road to goodness and happiness you can get before Father comes home."

"What are our burdens, Mother?" asked Amy.

"Each of you told what your burden was just now, except Beth," said her mother.

Shy, quiet Beth said, "Mine is dishes and dusting, and envying girls with nice pianos, and being afraid of people."

"Let us do it," said Meg. "It is only another name for trying to be good. We *want* to be good, but it's hard work and we forget."

"I will always be here to guide you," said their warm, thoughtful mother.

Hannah, their housekeeper, cleared the table. Then the girls worked on their sewing jobs. At nine they stopped work and sang, as usual, before they went to bed. No one but Beth could get much music out of the old piano, but she had a way of softly touching the yellowed keys. It had become a household custom to sing in the evening, for Mother was a born singer. Her cheerful singing was the first and last sound the girls heard every day.

# CHAPTER TWO

## *Merry Christmas*

Jo was the first to wake in the gray dawn of Christmas morning. No stockings hung at the fireplace in their room, and for a moment she felt disappointed. Then winter sunshine crept in to touch the bright heads of her sisters with a Christmas greeting. Soon, all the girls were up and running downstairs with a basket of secret gifts.

"Where is Mother, Hannah?" asked Meg.

"Goodness only knows," said the housekeeper. "Some poor creature came a-beggin', and your ma went to see what was needed."

"She will be back soon, so have everything ready," said Meg, looking over the presents.

"My handkerchiefs look nice, don't they?" said Beth, looking proudly at her work.

A door slammed and steps sounded in the hall.

"There's Mother. Hide the basket!" cried Jo.

The basket of gifts went under the sofa. The girls went to the table, eager for breakfast.

"Merry Christmas, Marmee!" they all cried.

"Merry Christmas, little daughters! I'm glad to see you're ready for breakfast, but I have one word to say before we sit down. Not far from here lies a poor woman with a newborn baby. Six children huddle in one bed, for there is no fire. And they have nothing to eat. My girls, will you give the Hummels your breakfast as a Christmas present?"

The girls were all very hungry, and for a minute no one spoke. Then Jo exclaimed, "I'm so glad you came before we began!"

"May I help carry the things to the poor children?" asked Beth.

"*I* shall take the cream and the muffins," added Amy, giving up what she liked most.

Meg was already covering the pancakes.

"I thought you'd do it," said Mrs. March, smiling. "When we come back we will have bread and milk for breakfast, and make it up at dinner."

They arrived at a room with broken windows, no fire, a sick mother, and a group of pale children cuddled under one old quilt, trying to keep warm.

"It is good angels come to us!" said the woman, crying for joy.

"Funny angels in hoods and mittens," said Jo, and everyone laughed.

Hannah made a fire, and stuffed her own cloak into the broken windowpanes. Mrs. March gave the mother tea and broth. She dressed the little baby as tenderly as if it had been her own. The girls set the table, and fed the children like hungry birds.

That was a very happy breakfast, though the March ladies didn't get any of it. When they left the Hummels, the hungry little girls who gave away their breakfasts on Christmas morning were the merriest people in the city.

"That's loving our neighbor. I like it," said Meg, as they set out their presents while their mother was upstairs collecting clothes for the Hummels.

"She's coming! Play the piano, Beth! Open the door, Amy! Three cheers for Marmee!" cried Jo.

Their mother walked into the room and Meg led her to the seat of honor. Mrs. March was both surprised and touched by each of her presents. The slippers went on at once. A new handkerchief was slipped into her pocket, well scented with Amy's perfume. The nice gloves were a perfect fit.

Later that evening Hannah called the girls for supper. When they saw the table, they were amazed. There was ice cream and cake and fruit and four bouquets of flowers!

"Old Mr. Laurence from the big house next door sent all this," explained Mrs. March.

"The Laurence boy's grandfather? But we don't know him!" exclaimed Meg.

"Hannah told one of his servants about your breakfast party. It pleased him. He knew my father years ago," said their mother. "This afternoon he sent me a note to say how kind all of you were. So now you have a little feast at night to make up for the bread-and-milk breakfast."

"His grandson put it into his head, I know he did! I wish we could get to know him. But he's so shy," said Jo, as the plates went round. "Our cat ran away once, and he brought her back. He needs fun, I'm sure he does," she added.

"I like the boy's manners," said Marmee. "He brought the flowers himself, and I should have asked him in. He looked so sad as he went away. He seemed to have no fun of his own."

Beth nestled up to her. She whispered softly, "I wish I could send my fun to Father. I'm afraid he isn't having such a merry Christmas."

# CHAPTER THREE

## *The Laurence Boy*

"Jo! Jo! We have an invitation for tomorrow night!" cried Meg. She found Jo reading and eating apples in her favorite window seat with her pet rat. She read the note to Jo. " 'Mrs. Gardiner would be happy to see Miss Margaret and Miss Josephine at a dance on New Year's Eve.' What shall we wear?"

"You know we each only have one nice dress for parties," answered Jo. "Yours is as good as new, but I have a burn in the back of mine. What shall *I* do?"

"Sit still and keep your back out of sight. The front is all right," replied Meg.

On New Year's Eve there was a great deal of running up and down, and laughing and talking.

After a few mishaps, Meg was finished at last. With help from the entire family, Jo's hair was arranged and her dress put on. Meg's high-heeled shoes were very tight, though she would not admit it. Jo's nineteen hairpins all seemed stuck into her head.

The girls seldom went to parties, and so they were quite nervous as they walked down the road with Hannah. But Mrs. Gardiner greeted them kindly. Meg knew her daughter, Sallie, and was at her ease very soon. But Jo felt as much out of place as a colt in a flower garden.

Jo decided to hide behind a curtain in a hallway. When she ducked in, she was surprised to find herself face to face with the "Laurence boy."

"Dear me, I didn't know anyone was here!" stammered Jo. "Did I disturb you?"

"Not a bit. I only came here because I don't know many people and felt rather strange."

"So did I." The boy sat down and looked at his shoes, till Jo said, "You live near us, don't you?"

The boy laughed, "Only next door. How is your little run-away cat doing, Miss March?" His black eyes shone with fun.

"Nicely, thank you, Mr. Laurence," said Jo with a smile. "And thank you for the food at Christmas."

"Grandpa sent it, Miss March."

"But *you* gave him the idea. And I'm not Miss March—I'm only Jo."

"And I'm only Laurie. Do you like to dance, Miss Jo?" he asked.

"I do if there is plenty of room, and everyone is lively. In a place like this I'm sure to step on people's toes. I keep out of mischief and let Meg dance. Do you dance?"

"Sometimes. I've been in Europe a good many years, and haven't been out in company enough yet to know how you do things here."

They chatted until they felt like old friends. Jo took several good looks at Laurie. She wanted to be able to describe him to her sisters. She said to herself, "Curly black hair, brown skin, big black eyes. Handsome nose, fine teeth, small hands and feet. Taller than I am. Very polite, for a boy, and altogether jolly."

"I suppose you are going to college soon?" she asked him.

Laurie shrugged. "Not for a year or two."

"Are you but fifteen?" asked Jo, looking at the tall lad.

"Sixteen, next month."

"How I wish *I* was going to college! You don't look as if you like the idea."

"I hate it!"

"What *do* you like?"

"To live in Italy, and to enjoy myself in my own way."

Jo wanted very much to ask what his own way was, but his black eyebrows and serious look made her change the subject. "That's a splendid polka! Why don't you go and try it?"

"If you will come, too," he answered with a polite little bow. "There's a long hall out there, and we can dance grandly, and no one will see us. Please come."

Jo thanked him and gladly went. They had a grand polka, for Laurie danced well.

When it was time to leave, Jo found that Meg had sprained her ankle dancing in her high-heeled shoes. It was too painful to walk on all the way home—and it had started to rain. Laurie offered the use of his grandfather's carriage, which had just pulled up outside.

Laurie sat up top with the driver while Jo, Meg, and Hannah rode below. The ladies rolled away inside the carriage, feeling very festive and elegant.

"I had a wonderful time. Did you?" asked Jo. She rumpled up her hair, making herself comfortable.

"Yes, till I hurt myself," answered Meg. "What were you doing, hidden away there?"

Jo told her about her talk and her polka with the Laurence boy. By the time she had finished, they were home.

With many thanks, they said good-night to Laurie. They were hoping not to disturb anyone, but the instant their door creaked, two sleepy voices cried out:

"Tell about the party! Tell about the party!"

# CHAPTER FOUR

## *Burdens and Blessings*

"Oh, dear. It is so hard to go back to our duties," sighed Meg the morning after the party.

The holidays were now over.

"I wish it was Christmas or New Year's all the time. Wouldn't it be fun?" answered Jo, yawning.

"We wouldn't enjoy ourselves half so much. But it does seem so nice to go to parties and read and rest and not work," said Meg.

Everyone seemed rather out of sorts that morning. Beth had a headache and lay on the sofa, trying to comfort herself with the cat and three kittens. Amy was fretting because she hadn't learned her school lessons, and she couldn't find her boots. Jo whistled and made a great racket getting ready. Mrs. March was very busy trying to finish a letter, and Hannah had the grumps.

"There never was such a cross family!" cried Jo. She had just upset an inkstand, broken both boot strings, and sat down upon her hat.

"You're the crossest person in it!" said Amy.

"Girls, girls, do be quiet one minute!" cried Mrs. March.

"Good-bye, Marmee," called out Jo. "We may be rascals this morning, but we'll come home angels tonight! Come on, Meg."

Jo and Meg left together for their jobs. Jo went off to tend old Aunt March and Meg to be governess to the King children. They looked back at the corner, for their mother was always at the window, waving.

Meg had a small salary as a governess. She tried not to be envious, but she *did* wish for pretty things and a happy life. At the Kings' she saw the older sisters' dainty ball dresses and bouquets. She heard lively gossip about theaters, concerts, sleighing, and parties. Meg did not complain much, but she was often bitter. She had not yet learned to know how rich she was in the blessings of home and family.

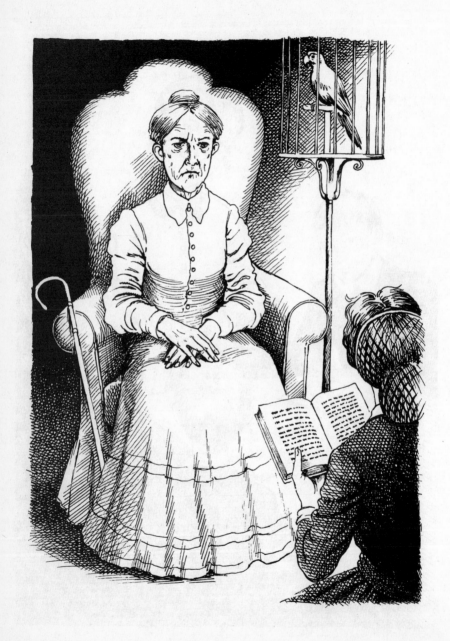

Jo happened to suit old Aunt March, who was lame and needed an active person to wait upon her. This did not suit Jo at all. But she got on very well thanks to a large library of fine books at Aunt March's house. Jo's greatest regret was that she couldn't read, run, and ride as much as she liked. A quick temper, sharp tongue, and restless spirit were always getting her into scrapes.

Beth was too bashful to go to school. She had tried, but suffered so much that it was given up. She did her lessons at home. She helped Hannah keep the home neat and comfortable. She was not lonely, for her world was filled with dolls, and she was by nature a busy bee. But she had her troubles as well. She longed very much to take music lessons and have a fine piano.

If anybody had asked Amy to name her greatest trial, she would have answered at once, "My nose." It was rather flat. Amy wanted a classic, straight nose, and drew whole sheets of handsome ones. She had a talent for drawing. She could also play twelve tunes, crochet, and read French without saying more than half of the words wrong. But things were seldom nice enough to please Amy. She was on her way to being a very spoiled little girl.

The two older girls took the younger sisters under their wings. Meg was Amy's closest friend, and Jo was gentle Beth's.

As the girls sat sewing that evening, Meg said, "Has anybody got anything to tell? It's been such a dismal day. I'm really dying for some amusement."

"I had a hard time with Aunt today," began Jo. "She is always so serious, and never lets herself have any fun. What a pleasant life she might have if only she chose! I don't envy her much, in spite of her money."

Meg said, "At the Kings' today I found everybody in a flurry. I was glad *I* didn't have any wild brothers to embarrass the family."

"I think being disgraced in school is a great deal *worser* than anything bad boys can do," said Amy. "Susie Perkins came to school today with a lovely red ring. I envied her so much. Till she got in trouble for drawing a picture of the teacher—and he took her by the ear—by the ear! Just imagine how horrid! I didn't envy her then."

Beth said, "I saw Mr. Laurence in the fish shop, but he didn't see me. He bought some fish for a poor woman who hadn't any dinner for her children. Wasn't it good of him?"

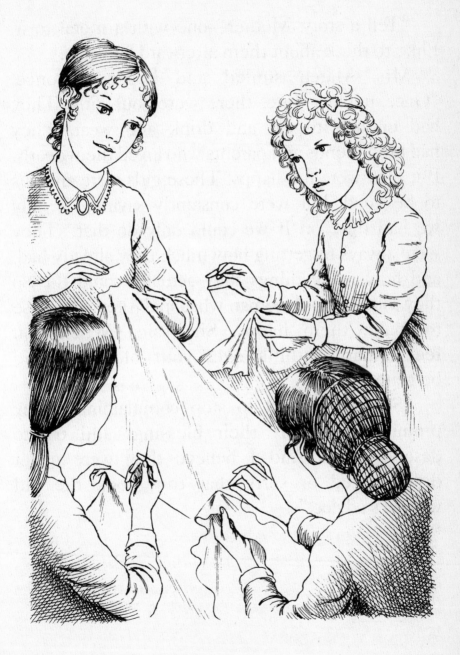

"Tell a story, Mother—one with a moral to it. I like to think about them afterward," said Jo.

Mrs. March smiled and began at once. "Once upon a time, there were four girls. They had enough to eat and drink and wear. They had kind friends and parents who loved them dearly. But they were not happy. These girls were anxious to be good, but were constantly saying, 'If only we had this,' or 'If we could only do that.' They were always forgetting how much they already had, and how many things they actually could do. So they asked an old woman what spell they could use to make them happy. She said, 'When you feel unhappy, think over your blessings, and be grateful.'

"So they agreed to stop complaining. They promised to enjoy their blessings and try to deserve them. And I believe they were never disappointed or sorry that they took the old woman's advice."

# CHAPTER FIVE

# *Being Neighborly*

A garden with a low hedge separated the Marches' house from that of Mr. Laurence. On one side was an old brown house. It was rather shabby without the vines and flowers that covered its walls in summer. On the other side was a stone mansion with a big coach house and neat lawns. Lovely things could be seen between the rich curtains.

Yet it seemed a lonely sort of house. No children played on the lawn. Few people went in and out. To Jo, this fine house next door seemed an enchanted palace. She had long wanted to see its glories and to know the Laurence boy. She had not seen him since the party.

"That boy needs to have fun," Jo said to herself as she walked by. "His grandpa does not know what's good for him, and keeps him shut up all alone to study."

She saw Mr. Laurence drive off. A curly black head was leaning on a thin hand at the upper window. "There he is," thought Jo. "Poor boy! All alone and looking sick this dismal day. I'll toss up a snowball and make him look out."

Up went a handful of soft snow, and the window opened at once. Jo laughed as she called out, "How do you do? Are you sick?"

Laurie leaned out and croaked, "Better, thank you. I've had a bad cold, and been shut up a week. It's dull up here."

"Isn't there some nice quiet girl who would amuse you?"

"Don't know any."

"You know us," laughed Jo. "I'm not quiet and nice, but I'll come."

Soon enough Jo appeared with a covered dish in one hand and Beth's three kittens in the other.

"What a cozy room this is," said Jo, looking around. "It only needs to have the hearth brushed and things straightened on the mantel. The books should be put here, and the pillows plumped up a bit. Now then, you're fixed." And so he was, for, as she laughed and talked, Jo had tidied the room.

"How kind you are!" Laurie said gratefully. "Now please let me do something to amuse you."

"No, I came to amuse *you*. Shall I read aloud?" and Jo looked toward some books nearby.

"Thank you, but I'd rather talk," said Laurie.

"I'll talk all day if you'll only set me going. Beth says I never know when to stop."

"Is Beth the rosy one who stays at home a good deal?" asked Laurie with interest.

"Yes, that's Beth."

"The pretty one is Meg, and the curly-haired one is Amy?"

"How did you find that out?"

Laurie blushed. "When I'm alone up here, I can't help looking over at your house. You always seem to be having such good times. It's like looking at a picture to see you all around the table with your mother. I haven't got any mother, you know." And Laurie poked the fire to hide a little twitching of the lips that he could not control.

The lonely look in his eyes went straight to Jo's warm heart. Laurie was sick and lonely. Feeling how rich she was in home and happiness, Jo gladly tried to share it with him.

"I wish you'd come over and see us," she said. "Mother would do you heaps of good, and Beth would sing to you, and Amy would dance. Meg and I would make you laugh, and we'd have jolly times. Wouldn't your grandpa let you?"

"I think he would, if your mother asked him. He's very kind, though he does not look so," Laurie said. "You see, Grandpa lives among his books. Mr. Brooke, my tutor, doesn't stay here. And I have no one to go around with, so I just stay home."

"You ought to go visiting. Then you'll have plenty of friends," said Jo.

Laurie offered to give Jo a tour of the house. He led the way from room to room until at last they came to the library. It was lined with books, and there were pictures and statues, and a great open fireplace.

"What richness!" sighed Jo, for she loved books. "Laurie, you ought to be the happiest boy in the world."

Laurie excused himself for a moment to see the doctor who had just arrived. Jo stood looking at a portrait of Mr. Laurence.

"I'm sure I wouldn't be afraid of him," she said out loud. "He's got kind eyes. He isn't as handsome as my grandfather, but I like him."

"Thank you, ma'am," said a gruff voice behind her. There, to her great dismay, stood old Mr. Laurence.

Poor Jo blushed, and her heart began to beat fast. The old gentleman said gruffly, "So you're not afraid of me, hey?"

"Not much, sir."

He gave a short laugh and shook her hand. "You've got your grandfather's spirit. He was a brave, honest man. I was proud to be his friend."

"Thank you, sir." And Jo was quite comfortable after that.

"What have you been doing to this boy of mine?" was the next question. "You think he needs cheering up a bit, do you?"

"Yes, sir, he seems a little lonely. Young folks would do him good. We are glad to help, for we don't forget the splendid Christmas present you sent us," said Jo.

Laurie returned, and Mr. Laurence noticed the change in his grandson as he talked and laughed with Jo. There was color, light, and life in the boy's face now. The girl was better than a doctor.

"She's right, the lad is lonely. I'll see what these little girls can do for him," thought Mr. Laurence.

They walked into the great drawing room. Jo noticed at once the grand piano.

"Do you play?" she asked, turning to Laurie. "I want to hear it, so I can tell Beth."

Laurie played and Jo listened. She wished Beth could hear him. She told Laurie how beautifully he played, and praised him so much that he blushed.

"That will do, young lady," interrupted the old man. "His music isn't bad, but I hope he will do as well in more important things. Going? I hope you'll come again. My respects to your mother. Good night, Doctor Jo." He shook hands kindly, but looked as if something did not please him.

When they got into the hall, Jo asked Laurie if she had said something wrong. He shook his head.

"No, it was me. He doesn't like to hear me play. Someday I'll tell you why. Thank you for coming."

"Well, take care, Laurie. Good night," said Jo.

"Good night, Jo, good night!"

When Jo had told her mother and sisters all about her visit with the neighbors, the family wished to go visiting at once. Mrs. March wanted to talk with the old gentleman because he had known her father. Meg longed to walk in the greenhouse. Beth sighed for the grand piano. Amy was eager to see the fine pictures and statues.

"Mother, why didn't Mr. Laurence like to have Laurie play the piano?" asked Jo.

"His son, Laurie's father, married an Italian lady. Mr. Laurence did not approve of her, even though she was a fine musician. He never saw his son after he married. They both died when Laurie was a little child. Laurie is like his mother and loves music. Perhaps his grandfather fears he may want to become a musician. At any rate, Laurie's skills must remind him of the woman he did not like."

"How silly!" said Jo. "Let him be a musician if he wants to."

# CHAPTER SIX

## Beth's Piano Lesson

The new friendship flourished like grass in spring. Everyone liked Laurie. And he told his tutor, Mr. Brooke, that "the Marches were splendid girls."

What good times they had—plays, sleigh rides, and skating parties. They had pleasant evenings in the Marches' old parlor, and little gatherings at the Laurences' great house. Meg walked in the greenhouse whenever she liked. Jo browsed over the new library. Amy copied pictures and enjoyed beauty to her heart's content.

Only Beth did not have the courage to visit. She went once with Jo, but the old gentleman stared at her so hard that she ran away.

But then Mr. Laurence mended matters. During one of his visits he started talking about Laurie's piano lessons and their grand piano. Beth found it impossible to stay in her distant corner. He said to Mrs. March, "Wouldn't some of your girls like to practice on the piano now and then, ma'am?"

Here he rose, as if to leave. A little hand slipped into his, and Beth looked up at him and said, "Oh, sir, they would—very, very much!"

"Are you the musical girl?" he asked. He looked down at her kindly.

"I'm Beth. I love music dearly. I'll come, if you are quite sure nobody will be disturbed."

"The house is empty half the day, so come as much as you like. I'll leave the side door open."

Beth gave the hand a grateful squeeze. The old gentleman kissed her cheek, saying softly, "I had a little girl once, with eyes like these. God bless you, my dear!" He went away in a great hurry.

Next day, Beth made her way like a mouse to the side door of the Laurences' house and into the drawing room. Quite by accident, of course, some easy music lay on the piano. With trembling fingers, Beth touched the keys. She immediately forgot everything but the happiness the music gave her.

After that, Beth played nearly every day. She never knew that Mr. Laurence opened his study door to hear the music. She never saw Laurie warn the servants away. She never suspected that the new music she found on the piano was put there for her. She simply enjoyed herself. And because she was so grateful for *this* blessing, a *greater* blessing was given to her.

Beth made Mr. Laurence some slippers as a thank-you gift. Several days passed after she and Laurie smuggled them into the study, but the old gentleman had said nothing about them. Then, one afternoon, Beth went out to do an errand. On her return, she saw four heads popping in and out of the parlor windows. Several hands waved, and joyful voices screamed.

"Here's a letter from the old gentleman! Come quick, and read it!"

At the door her sisters pulled her inside. Beth turned pale with delight and surprise. There stood a little piano, with a letter lying on the glossy lid.

"For me?" gasped Beth, holding onto Jo. "You read it! I can't. Oh, it is too lovely!"

Jo opened the paper and read:

*Dear Madam—*

*I have had many pairs of slippers in my life, but never any I liked as much as yours. They will always remind me of you. I am sending you something which once belonged to the little granddaughter I lost. With hearty thanks and best wishes.*

*James Laurence*

"You'll have to go and thank him," said Jo, but she was joking. She knew that shy Beth would never be able to face the old gentleman.

"Yes. I guess I'll go now, before I get frightened," Beth said. And then, to her family's surprise, she boldly walked next door to the Laurences' house.

They would have been still more amazed if they had seen what Beth did afterward. She knocked at the study door, went right up to Mr. Laurence, and held out her hand. Remembering that he had lost the little girl he loved, she put both arms round his neck and kissed his cheek.

Beth ceased to fear Mr. Laurence at that moment. She learned that love is more powerful than fear.

# CHAPTER SEVEN

# Amy Learns a Sour Lesson

"I hate being in debt," Amy said.

"In debt? What do you mean?" Meg asked.

Amy explained that the girls at school were giving out limes at recess. If one girl liked another girl, she gave her a lime. Amy had been given many, but hadn't any limes to share in return.

"How much money do you need?" asked Meg, taking out her purse.

"A quarter would more than do it." Meg handed her the money. "Oh, thank you! I'll have a grand feast, for I haven't tasted a lime this week."

Next day a rumor went round school that Amy March had twenty-four delicious limes and was going to treat her friends. Amy became quite the show-off as she displayed her great wealth of limes.

Jenny Snow was a young lady who had picked on Amy for not having limes before. *Now* she wanted to be friends again. But Amy had not forgotten the way Jenny had treated her. She said, "You needn't be so polite all of a sudden. You won't get any limes from me."

This made Jenny very angry. She quickly informed Mr. Davis, the teacher, that Amy had limes in her desk.

Now Mr. Davis had announced that no limes were to be in the classroom. He had promised to use his ruler on the first person to break the rules.

"Miss March, come here. Bring with you the limes you have in your desk."

Amy took out the limes and laid them before Mr. Davis.

"Now take these disgusting things and throw them out of the window."

Amy was red with shame and anger. She went to and fro six dreadful times. As she returned from her last trip, Mr. Davis said, "I am sorry this has happened, but I never allow my rules to be broken. Miss March, hold out your hand."

Too proud to cry or beg, Amy threw back her head bravely. She did not flinch as several tingling blows landed on her little palm. They did not hurt, but that made no difference. For the first time in her life, she had been struck. The disgrace was as deep as if he had knocked her down.

"You will now stand on the platform till recess," said Mr. Davis.

During the fifteen minutes that followed, the proud and sensitive little girl suffered a shame and pain which she never forgot. During the twelve years of her life she had been governed by love alone. Though both her hand and her heart ached, it was more painful to think of home. She thought, "They will be so disappointed in me!"

She was in a sad state when she got home. Her family did their best to comfort her, but Amy insisted that she would never return to school.

"Well, you can have a vacation. But I want you to study a little every day with Beth," said Mrs. March.

"That's good! It's terrible to think of those lovely limes," sighed Amy.

"I am not sorry you lost them. You broke the rules, and deserved some punishment," said Mrs. March. "But I do not agree with Mr. Davis's method."

"Are you glad I was disgraced before the whole school?" cried Amy.

"You are getting to be rather conceited, my dear. It's time you tried to correct it," replied her mother. "You have a good many little gifts. But there is no need of showing them off."

Amy was quiet for a moment. Then she asked, "Is Laurie a talented boy?"

"Yes. He has had an excellent education. And he has much talent," replied her mother.

"And he isn't stuck-up, is he?" asked Amy.

"Not in the least. That is why he is so charming and we all like him so much."

"I see. It's nice to have talents and be elegant. But it's not nice to show off," said Amy thoughtfully.

"Any more than it's proper to wear all your bonnets and gowns and ribbons at once—just so folks may know you've got them," added Jo. And the lesson ended in a laugh.

# CHAPTER EIGHT

## *Jo Finds Some Weak Spots*

"Tell me where you are going!" cried Amy one Saturday afternoon. Meg and Jo were getting ready to go out. "You might let *me* go. I haven't got anything to do."

"I can't, dear, because you aren't invited..." began Meg.

But Jo broke in impatiently, "You *can't* go, Amy. So don't be a baby and whine about it."

"You are going somewhere with Laurie, aren't you? Are you going to see a play at the theater?"

"Yes, we are. Now stop bothering us," said Jo.

"Please let me go," pleaded Amy.

"Suppose we take her..." began Meg.

"If she goes *I* won't, and if I don't, *Laurie* won't like it. I would think she'd hate to poke herself in where she isn't wanted," said Jo crossly.

When Laurie called, the two girls hurried down and left their sister crying. As the three set out, Amy called out in a threatening tone, *"You'll be sorry for this, Jo March!"*

Laurie, Jo, and Meg had a charming time, for the play was wonderful. But Jo's pleasure had a drop of bitterness in it. She wondered what her sister would do to make her "sorry."

When they got home, they found Amy reading in the parlor. Jo searched for evidence of Amy's revenge, but everything was in its place. She decided that Amy had forgiven her.

There Jo was mistaken. The next day she made a discovery that produced a storm. Meg, Beth, and Amy were sitting together late in the afternoon when Jo burst into the room. "Has anyone taken my writing book?" she demanded. Meg and Beth said "no" at once, and looked surprised. Amy said nothing. Jo was on her in a minute.

"Amy, you've got it!"

"You'll never see your silly old book again," cried Amy. "I burned it up."

"What! My book I was so fond of, and meant to finish writing before Father got home? Have you really burned it?" said Jo, turning very pale.

"Yes, I did! I told you I'd make you pay yesterday, and I have, so…"

Jo's hot temper took over. She shook Amy till her teeth chattered in her head. "You wicked girl! I never can write it again. I'll never forgive you as long as I live."

When Mrs. March came home she made Amy realize the wrong she had done her sister. Jo's book was the pride of her heart. It was only half a dozen little fairy tales, but Jo had put her whole heart into her work. She had hoped to make something good enough to print. Amy's bonfire had destroyed the loving work of several years.

When the tea bell rang, Jo appeared, looking grim. It took all of Amy's courage to say, "Please forgive me, Jo. I'm very, very sorry."

"I never shall forgive you," was Jo's answer. And from that moment, she ignored Amy entirely.

Next day, Jo still looked like a thunder cloud. "I'll ask Laurie to go skating. He is always kind and jolly," said Jo to herself, and off she went. But Amy heard the clash of skates.

"This is the last ice we shall have," pouted Amy. "But it's no use to ask such a grump to take me."

Meg said, "Go after them. Once Laurie has cheered her up, I'm sure she'll be your friend again."

"I'll try," said Amy.

It was not far to the river. Jo saw Amy coming, and turned her back. Laurie did not see, for he was carefully skating along the shore, testing the ice.

"I'll go on to see if it's all right before we begin to race," Amy heard him say. Jo heard Amy panting after her and so she skated slowly down the river away from Amy.

As Laurie turned the bend, he shouted back, "Keep near the shore. It isn't safe in the middle."

Jo heard, but Amy had not. Jo glanced over her shoulder. "Let her take care of herself," she thought.

Amy skated out toward the smoother ice in the middle of the river. For a minute Jo stood still with a strange feeling in her heart. Then something turned her around—just in time to see Amy go down, with a sudden crash of weak ice and a cry that made Jo's heart freeze.

Jo tried to rush forward, but her feet had no strength. Something rushed swiftly by her, and Laurie's voice cried out, "Bring a rail. Quick!"

Lying flat, Laurie held Amy up by his arm and a hockey stick till Jo dragged a rail from the fence. Together they got the child out, more frightened than hurt. Shivering, dripping, and crying, they got Amy home.

Later, when the house was quiet, Jo went to her mother and said, "If Amy should die, Mother, it would be my fault." She dropped down beside the bed in tears. "It's my dreadful temper! I try to cure it, and then it breaks out worse than ever. Oh, Mother, what shall I do?" cried poor Jo.

"Remember this day, and resolve that you will never know another like it," her mother said. "You think your temper is the worst, but mine used to be just like it."

"Yours, Mother? Why, you are never angry!"

"Your father helped me to control my temper, Jo. He showed me that I must try to practice all the virtues I want my little girls to have."

"Oh, Mother, if I'm ever half as good as you, I'll be satisfied," cried Jo. "I let the sun go down on my anger yesterday. I wouldn't forgive Amy, and today it might have been too late!" She leaned over her sister, softly stroking the wet hair scattered on the pillow.

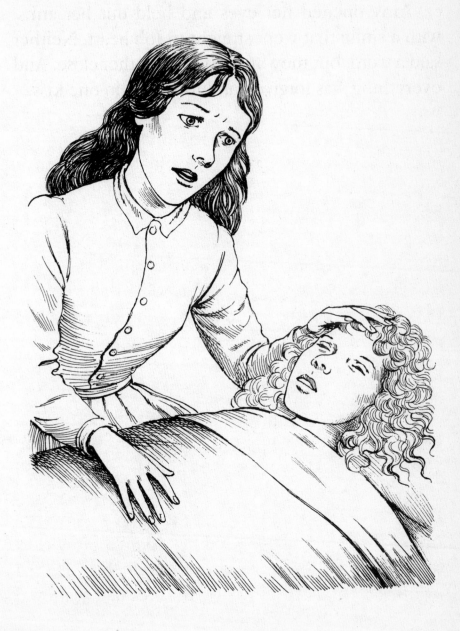

Amy opened her eyes and held out her arms, with a smile that went straight to Jo's heart. Neither said a word, but they hugged one another close. And everything was forgiven and forgotten in one kiss.

# CHAPTER NINE

## Meg Has a Beauty Lesson

Meg stood packing her trunk one April day. She had been invited to spend two weeks in the country with Annie Moffat and her family. Sallie Gardiner was going as well.

"What did Mother give you out of the treasure box?" asked Amy. The treasure box was a cedar chest in which Mrs. March kept a few old valuables. They were presented as gifts for her girls when the proper time came.

"A pair of silk stockings, that pretty carved fan, and a lovely blue sash. I wanted the violet silk dress, but there isn't time to fix it."

"You've got your white dress for the big party.

You always look like an angel in white," said Amy.

"It will have to do," Meg returned. She looked at her well-worn wardrobe and sighed. "I wonder if I shall *ever* have real lace on my clothes and bows on my caps?"

"You said the other day that you'd be perfectly happy if you could only go to Annie Moffat's," observed Beth in her quiet way.

"So I did! Well, I *am* happy, and I *won't* fret. But it does seem as if the more one gets the more one wants, doesn't it?"

The next day, Meg departed in style for two weeks of pleasure. The Moffats were very fashionable. Simple Meg was rather overwhelmed at first. Everything was so splendid and elegant. But the Moffats were kind people, and soon put their guest at her ease.

Meg certainly liked having nothing to do but enjoy herself. She began to act and talk just like the rich girls around her. The more she saw of Annie's pretty things, the more she sighed to be rich. Home now looked bare and dismal as she thought of it.

It didn't take long for Meg to notice that her own clothing was old and shabby. Annie and her sisters wore only the finest dresses. No one said a word about it, but Meg's heart felt very heavy. She had a gentle heart, but she was also very proud.

Poor Meg did not sleep well after a small party one evening. She got up heavy-eyed and unhappy. That afternoon, Annie's oldest sister, Belle, announced to Meg that she had invited "young Mr. Laurence" to the next big party.

"What shall you wear?" asked Sallie Gardiner.

"My old white dress again," said Meg. She tried to speak quite easily, but felt very uncomfortable.

Belle said kindly, "I've got a sweet blue silk packed away, which I've outgrown. Wear it to please me, won't you?"

"You are very kind. But I don't mind my old dress if you don't," said Meg.

"Now, do let me please myself by dressing you up in style. You'd be a regular little beauty with a touch here and there," said Belle.

Meg agreed. She very much wanted to see if she would be "a little beauty" after some touching up. The excitement caused her to forget all her uncomfortable feelings toward the Moffats.

Belle and her maid turned Meg into a fine lady. They crimped and curled her hair and reddened her lips. They laced her into a sky-blue dress, which was so tight she could hardly breathe. Silver jewelry was added, and a pair of high-heeled silk boots granted the last wish of her heart. A lace handkerchief, a fan, and a bouquet finished her off. Belle proudly looked over her newly dressed doll.

Meg got safely downstairs and into the drawing rooms where the guests had gathered. She very soon discovered that there is a charm about fine clothes. People who had ignored her before were suddenly very polite to her. Young boys asked to meet her.

But soon the tight dress gave her a side-ache. Her skirt kept getting under her feet. And she was afraid she was going to lose or break one of the silver earrings. Then she suddenly saw Laurie. He was staring at her with surprise and disapproval. Something in his honest eyes made her wish she had her old dress on.

Meg crossed the room to shake hands with her friend. "I was afraid you wouldn't come," she said.

"Jo wanted me to come, and tell her how you looked," answered Laurie.

"What shall you tell her?" asked Meg, full of curiosity to know his opinion of her.

"I shall say I didn't know you. For you look so grown-up and unlike yourself, I'm quite afraid of you," he said. "I don't like fuss and feathers."

That was altogether too much from a lad younger than herself. Meg walked away, saying, "You are the rudest boy I ever saw."

She went and stood at a quiet window to cool her cheeks. As she stood there, some of the party guests walked by, but did not see her standing there. Meg heard one of the men say: "They are making such a fool of that March girl. She's made up to look like a doll tonight."

"Oh, dear!" sighed Meg. "I wish I'd been sensible and worn my own things."

Turning, she saw Laurie. He said, "Please forgive my rudeness. Come and dance with me. I don't like your gown, but I do think you are just splendid."

Meg smiled. She whispered, "Take care my skirt doesn't trip you up. I was a goose to wear it."

After the dance, Laurie did not speak to Meg again till suppertime, when he saw her drinking champagne and flirting with Annie's brothers.

"You'll have a splitting headache tomorrow if you drink much of that," he whispered, leaning over her chair.

"I'm not Meg tonight; I'm 'a doll' who does all sorts of crazy things. Tomorrow I shall be good again," she answered.

"Wish tomorrow was here, then," muttered Laurie, unhappy with the change in Meg.

Meg was sick all the next day. On Saturday she went home, feeling that she had "sat in the lap of luxury" long enough. On Sunday evening, she sat with her mother and Jo, saying very little. Then, as the clock struck nine, Meg went to her mother's side, saying bravely, "Marmee, I want to confess."

"I thought so. What is it, dear?"

She told them how the Moffat girls had dressed her up like a doll, and how she had been flattered by the attention. She also confessed to drinking champagne and trying to flirt. Jo saw her mother fold her lips tightly.

Mrs. March said gravely, "I was very unwise to let you go."

"I won't let it hurt me, Mother."

"Learn to know and value the praise which is worth having, Meg."

Meg sighed. "Poor girls don't stand any chance, Belle says."

"Then we'll be old maids," said Jo.

Mrs. March held her daughters' hands. "My dear girls, you do not have to marry rich men merely because they are rich. I'd rather see you poor men's wives, if you were happy, than queens on thrones, without self-respect and peace.

"One thing to remember, my girls: Mother is always ready to be your listening ear, and Father to be your friend. And both of us hope that our daughters will be the pride and comfort of our lives."

"We will, Marmee, we will!" cried both, with all their hearts.

# CHAPTER TEN

# Spring Ends – And Play Begins

"The first of June! The Kings are off to the seashore tomorrow, and I'm free. Three months' vacation. How I shall enjoy it!" exclaimed Meg.

"Aunt March went today, too!" said Jo. "I was afraid she'd ask me to go with her."

"What shall you do all vacation?" asked Amy.

"I'm going to rest and play to my heart's content," replied Meg.

Jo said, "I'm going to read in the old apple tree."

"Let's not do any lessons for a while, Beth. Let's play all the time and rest," proposed Amy.

"Well, I will, if Mother doesn't mind. I want to learn some new songs," admitted Beth.

"May we, Mother?" asked Meg. Mrs. March sat sewing in the corner.

"You may try your experiment for a week and see how you like it. I think by Saturday night you will find that all play and no work is as bad as all work and no play."

They began by lounging for the rest of the day. Next morning, Meg did not appear till ten o'clock. The room seemed lonely and untidy. Jo had not filled the vases, Beth had not dusted, and Amy's books lay scattered about. Nothing was neat and pleasant but Marmee's corner.

Jo spent the morning on the river with Laurie and the afternoon reading up in the apple tree. Beth went to her music. Amy sat down to draw under the honeysuckle. She got caught in a rain shower and came home dripping. Meg went shopping in the afternoon.

At tea time they met to discuss their day. Meg had discovered her new dress would shrink in the wash. Jo had sunburned her nose and had a raging headache. Beth was weary from learning three or four songs at once. Amy deeply regretted the rain damage done to her dress.

But these were small troubles. They assured

their mother that the experiment was working fine. She smiled and said nothing. With Hannah's help she did their neglected work.

It was amazing how uncomfortable things became. The days got longer and longer. Everyone felt uneasy. Meg spoiled her clothes in her attempts to fancy them up. Jo got so fidgety that even Laurie quarreled with her. Beth got on pretty well, for she was constantly forgetting that it was to be *all play and no work*. Amy fared worst of all. She didn't like dolls, fairy tales were childish, and one couldn't draw *all* the time.

By Friday night each was glad the week was nearly done. Hoping to help them learn their lesson more deeply, Mrs. March gave Hannah a vacation. She wanted the girls to enjoy the full effect of the experiment. When they got up Saturday morning, there was no fire in the kitchen, and no breakfast in the dining room. Their mother was nowhere to be seen.

"Mercy on us! What *has* happened?" cried Jo.

"Mother says she is going to stay quietly in her room all day," said Meg, coming downstairs. "She says it has been a hard week for her. We must take care of ourselves."

It was an immense relief to have a little work. There was plenty of food in the pantry. While Beth and Amy set the table, Meg made breakfast.

Jo took a tray up to their mother. The boiled tea was very bitter, the omelet scorched, and the biscuits tough. But Mrs. March received them with thanks. She laughed heartily after Jo was gone.

Many were the complaints below about the awful breakfast. "Never mind, I'll get the lunch," said Jo, who knew less than Meg about cooking. With perfect faith in her own powers as a chef, she immediately invited Laurie to lunch.

Jo walked to the market. She was sure she made very good bargains. She bought a very young lobster, some very old asparagus, and two boxes of unripe strawberries.

Mrs. March went out, after peeping here and there to see how matters went. A strange sense of helplessness fell upon the girls as the gray bonnet vanished round the corner.

Words cannot describe Jo's attempts at cooking. She boiled the asparagus until the tops fell apart. The bread burned black. She hammered and poked the little lobster and hid the small bits of meat in lettuce leaves. The potatoes were not done.

"It's terrible to spend your whole morning for nothing," thought Jo. She rang the bell half an hour later than usual.

One thing after another was tasted and left on the plates. Amy giggled and Meg looked distressed. Laurie talked and laughed to give a cheerful tone to the scene.

Jo's one strong point was the fruit. She knew she had sugared it well, and had a pitcher of rich cream to eat with it. She glanced at Laurie. There was a slight pucker around his mouth. Amy took a heaping spoonful, choked, hid her face in her napkin, and left the table quickly.

"Oh, what is it?" exclaimed Jo.

"Salt instead of sugar, and the cream is sour," replied Meg.

Jo uttered a groan and fell back in her chair. She was on the verge of crying when she met Laurie's eyes, which looked merry. The comical side of the affair suddenly struck her, and she laughed till tears ran down her cheeks. The unfortunate lunch ended happily, with bread and butter, olives and fun.

As twilight fell, the girls gathered on the porch where the June roses were budding beautifully. Each groaned or sighed as she sat down, as if tired or troubled.

"Are you pleased with your experiment, girls?" Marmee asked, as Beth nestled up to her. They each turned toward Mother with brightening faces, as flowers turn toward the sun.

"Not me!" cried Jo decidedly.

"Nor I," echoed the others.

"You think that it is better to have a few duties and live a little for others, do you?"

"Lounging doesn't pay," observed Jo. "I'm tired of it."

"Work is wholesome," Marmee said. "It keeps us from mischief, is good for health and spirits, and gives us a sense of independence."

"We'll work like busy bees, see if we don't," said Jo. "I'll learn cooking, and my next dinner party will be a success."

"I'll make a set of shirts for Father. That will be better than fussing over my own things," said Meg.

"I'll do my lessons every day, and not spend so much time with my music," said Beth.

Amy followed their example by declaring, "I shall learn to make buttonholes, and attend to my grammar lessons."

"Very good! Then I am quite satisfied with the experiment. Remember to have regular hours for work and play, and make each day both useful and pleasant."

"We'll remember, Mother!"
And they did.

# CHAPTER ELEVEN

# A *Summer Picnic*

Laurie invited the March girls to join him on a picnic. Some friends of his from England were visiting, and he hoped to show them a grand time.

Jo flew in to tell the news. "Of course we can go—Mother? Laurie's tutor, Mr. Brooke, is going as the chaperone. Ned Moffat and Sallie Gardiner are coming, too. I can row, and Meg can see to lunch."

"Do you know anything about the English family, Jo?" asked Meg.

"Only that there are four of them. Kate is older than you. Fred and Frank—twins—are about my age. And there is a little girl, Grace, who is nine or ten. Laurie knew them in Europe."

Jo turned to her sister. "You'll come, Bethy?"

"If you won't let any boys talk to me. I like to please Laurie, and I'm not afraid of Mr. Brooke, he is so kind. But I don't want to play, or sing, or say anything."

"That's my good girl. You do try to fight off your shyness, and I love you for it. Fighting faults isn't easy, as I know. Now let's do double duty today, so that we can play tomorrow with free minds," said Jo, picking up a broom.

The sun peeped into the girls' room early next morning, and soon a lively bustle began in both houses. Beth kept looking out the window and reporting what went on next door.

"There goes the man with the tent! Now Mr. Laurence is looking up at the sky. I wish he would go, too. There's Laurie, looking like a sailor! Oh, here's a carriage full of people—a tall lady, a little girl, and two dreadful boys. One is lame. Poor thing, he's got a crutch. Be quick, girls! It's getting late."

Jo marched straight away and the rest followed. They were a bright little band of sisters, all looking their best in summer suits, with happy faces under their bouncy hat brims.

Laurie ran to meet the girls and present them to his friends. Meg was grateful to see that Miss Kate was dressed simply. Jo thought Kate had a stand-off-don't-touch-me air. Beth decided that the lame boy, Frank, was not "dreadful," but gentle, and she would be kind to him. Amy found Grace a well-mannered, merry little person. After staring at one another for a few minutes, they suddenly became very good friends.

The group set off in two rowboats, and Fred manned a wherry boat. It was not far to the picnic field. The tent was pitched and the croquet wickets were down by the time they arrived.

"Welcome to Camp Laurence!" said the young host as they landed with exclamations of delight. "Let's have a game before it gets hot, and then we'll see about dinner."

Frank, Beth, Amy, and Grace sat down to watch the game played by the other eight. Mr. Brooke chose Meg, Kate, and Fred. Laurie took Sallie, Jo, and Ned. The English played well, but the Americans played better.

Fred cheated a bit, and Jo got angry, but managed to keep her temper. Both Meg and Laurie praised her for it.

Mr. Brooke, who was Laurie's tutor, had come along to watch over the young crowd. Meg had noticed that he was an intelligent, warm man with handsome brown eyes.

Mr. Brooke looked at his watch and announced, "Time for lunch."

A very merry lunch it was, for everything seemed fresh and funny.

"What shall we do when we can't eat any more?" asked Laurie.

"Have games till it's cooler," returned Jo. "I dare say Miss Kate knows something new and nice. Go and ask her. She's company, and you ought to stay with her more."

"Aren't you company, too? I thought Kate would suit Brooke, but he keeps talking to Meg."

Miss Kate *did* know several new games. They first tried something called Rig-marole. One person began a story, and told it as long as they pleased. Then, just at some exciting point, the next person took over the story. The happy group told a most outrageous and interesting story. Afterward, the elders—Meg, Kate, and Mr. Brooke—sat together on the grass. Miss Kate took out her sketch book.

"I wish I could draw," said Meg.

"Why don't you learn?" returned Miss Kate.

"I haven't time."

"I took a few lessons privately. Can't you do the same with your governess?"

"I have none. I am a governess myself."

"Oh, indeed!" said Miss Kate. But she might as well have said, "Dear me, how dreadful!"

Mr. Brooke looked up and said quickly, "Young ladies in America are admired and respected for supporting themselves."

"Oh, yes, of course it's very nice and proper in America for them to do so," said Miss Kate in a rather rude voice.

Mr. Brooke had recently translated a German song for Meg, and he asked her if she had found his work useful. The two of them studied a little book of German poetry together. Miss Kate watched them closely. Then she shut her sketchbook, saying, "I must look after Grace." She strolled away, adding to herself, "What odd people these Yankees are. I'm afraid Laurie will be quite spoiled among them."

"I forgot that English people turn up their noses at governesses," said Meg to Mr. Brooke when Kate had left.

"There's no place like America for us workers, Miss Margaret," said Mr. Brooke, looking quite cheerful.

"I'm glad I live in it then. I only wish I liked teaching as you do."

"I think you would if you had Laurie for a student. I shall be very sorry to lose him next year," said Mr. Brooke.

"Going to college, I suppose?" Meg's lips asked that question, but her eyes added, "And what becomes of you?"

"Yes, it's high time he went. As soon as he is off, I shall become a soldier."

"I am glad of that!" exclaimed Meg. "I should think every young man would want to go help in the war. Though it is hard for the mothers and sisters who stay at home," she added sorrowfully.

"I have no mother or sisters," said Mr. Brooke in a quiet voice.

"Laurie and his grandfather would care a great deal if you went. And we would all be very sorry to have any harm happen to you," said Meg, looking into those handsome brown eyes.

"Thank you," returned Mr. Brooke, looking into Meg's eyes, and becoming cheerful again.

Another game of croquet finished the afternoon. At sunset the tent was taken down, baskets packed, wickets pulled up, and boats loaded. The whole party floated down the river, singing at the tops of their voices.

On the lawn where it had gathered, the little party separated. As the four sisters went home through the garden, Miss Kate looked after them. She said quite smugly, "In spite of their strange manners, American girls are very nice when one knows them."

"I quite agree with you," said Mr. Brooke.

# CHAPTER TWELVE

## *Castles in the Air*

Laurie was swinging in his hammock one warm September afternoon when he saw the Marches going out on some journey.

"Well, that's cool," said Laurie to himself. "To have a picnic and never ask me! I'll see what's going on."

He topped the hill the girls had climbed and peeped through the bushes. "Here's a scene!" he said to himself.

It *was* a pretty picture. The sisters sat together in a shady nook, with sun and shadow flickering over them. The wind lifted their hair and cooled their hot cheeks. Meg sat sewing daintily and looking as fresh

and sweet as a rose. Beth was sorting pinecones, for she made pretty things with them. Amy was sketching a group of ferns. Jo was knitting as she read aloud.

"May I come in, please? Or shall I be a bother?" Laurie asked, advancing slowly.

Meg lifted her eyebrows, but Jo scowled at her. She said at once, "Of course you may. We should have asked you before, only we thought you wouldn't care for such a girl's game."

"I always like your games. But if Meg doesn't want me, I'll go away."

"I don't mind, if you do something. It's against the rules to be lazy here. If you want to join the 'Busy Bee Society,' you must be useful," said Meg.

"Mother likes to have us out-of-doors as much as possible. We bring our work here and have nice times," said Jo. "From this hill we can see far away to the place where we hope to live sometime."

Jo pointed, and Laurie sat up to examine. Through an opening in the wood one could look across the wide, blue river, far over the outskirts of the great city, to the green hills that rose to meet the sky. The sun was low, and the heavens glowed with the beauty of an autumn sunset.

"How beautiful that is!" said Laurie softly.

"Wouldn't it be fun if all our dreams and castles in the air could come true, and we could live in them?" said Jo.

"I'd be a famous musician," said Laurie. "And I'd never be bothered about money or business. I'd just enjoy myself and live for what I like. That's my favorite castle. What's yours, Meg?"

Meg found it hard to tell hers. She said slowly, "I would like a lovely house, full of beautiful things. Nice food, pretty clothes, handsome furniture, and heaps of money. How I should enjoy it!"

Jo said, "I want to do something heroic or wonderful that won't be forgotten after I'm dead. I think I shall write books, and get rich and famous. That would suit me, so that is *my* favorite dream."

"Mine is to stay at home safe, and help take care of the family," said Beth with a content smile. "Since I have my little piano, I am perfectly satisfied. I only wish we may all keep well and be together. Nothing else."

"I have ever so many wishes. But my favorite is to be an artist, and go to Rome. I'll do fine pictures, and be the best artist in the whole world," was Amy's modest desire.

"In ten years let's meet, and see how many of us have got our wishes. Or how much nearer we are then than now," said Jo.

"I hope I shall have done something to be proud of by that time. But I'm such a lazy dog," Laurie admitted. "Grandfather wants me to be a businessman, and I'd rather be shot."

Meg said in her most motherly tone, "Do your best at college, Laurie. Then your grandfather won't be unfair to you. Do your duty and you'll get your reward by being respected and loved. Good Mr. Brooke has done his duty, and he will be rewarded in some way, I'm sure."

"What do *you* know about Mr. Brooke?" asked Laurie. His black eyes twinkled slyly.

Meg blushed. "Only what your grandpa told us about him. He took care of his own mother till she died. Now he helps to support the old woman who nursed his mother. He is just as generous and patient and good as he can be."

"So he is, dear fellow!" said Laurie heartily. "It's like Grandpa to find out all about him, and to tell his goodness to others. If ever I do get my wish, you'll see what I do for Brooke."

Laurie squeezed Meg's kind little hand. To show he was not offended by her lecture, he wound yarn for her. Then he recited poetry to please Jo, shook down cones for Beth, and helped Amy with her ferns. In all, he proved himself well fit for the "Busy Bee Society."

That night, when Beth played the piano for Mr. Laurence, Laurie watched the old man, who sat with his gray head on his hand.

The boy said to himself, "I'll let my castle go, and stay with the dear old gentleman while he needs me. I am all he has."

# CHAPTER THIRTEEN

## *Autumn Secrets*

The autumn sun lay warmly in the high window. Jo was seated on the old sofa in the attic, writing busily, her papers spread out before her.

She scribbled away till the last page was filled, then signed her name with a fancy flair. She threw down her pen, and exclaimed, "There, I've done my best!"

Jo tied the papers up with a red ribbon. She took another set of papers from the cupboard, and put both in her pocket. Then she crept downstairs.

Very quietly, Jo put on her hat and jacket. Going to the back window, she got out on the roof of a low porch. She swung herself down and took a roundabout way to the road. Once there, she hailed a passing carriage-bus. She looked very merry and mysterious as it rolled away.

The bus let her off in town, and after a few wrong turns, she found the place she was looking for. She went into the doorway and looked up the dirty stairs. After standing still a minute, she suddenly walked away. She went back, stood, and walked away again several times. This greatly amused a black-eyed young gentleman who was watching her from the window of a building across the street. Finally Jo gave herself a shake, pulled her hat over her eyes, and walked up the stairs. She looked scared and nervous, as if she were going to have all her teeth out.

There was a dentist's sign, among others, at the entrance to the building. The young gentleman stared at the sign for a moment. Then he put on his coat and went down to wait in the doorway.

In ten minutes Jo came running downstairs with a very red face. When she saw the young gentleman she looked anything but pleased. He asked, "Did you have a bad time?"

"Not very."

"How many did you have out?"

Jo looked at her friend as if she did not understand him, then began to laugh. He thought she had been to the dentist!

"What are you laughing at?" said Laurie.

They walked in silence a few minutes. Then Laurie said, "I'd like to tell you something very interesting. It's a secret. If I tell you, you must tell me *your* secret."

Jo thought about this for a moment. Then she whispered, "Well, I've left two stories with a newspaper man to see if he'll print them. He will give me his answer next week."

"Hooray for Miss March, the famous American author!" cried Laurie. "Your stories are works of Shakespeare compared to half the rubbish that is published every day."

Jo's eyes sparkled. "And what's *your* secret?"

"I know where Meg's other glove is."

"Is that all?" said Jo, looking disappointed. Meg had left a pair of gloves at the Laurences' house weeks ago. Only one had ever been found. Laurie nodded with a face full of mystery. "All right, Laurie, tell then. Where's the glove?"

Laurie bent, and whispered three words in Jo's ear. She looked shocked and quite displeased.

"How do you know?" Jo said sharply.

"Saw it in his pocket. Isn't it romantic?"

"No! It's horrid!"

"Don't you like the secret?"

"Of course I don't. The idea of anybody coming to take Meg away! No, thank you," said Jo rather ungratefully. She tried to hide the trembling of her lips. Lately she had felt that Meg was getting to be a woman, and Laurie's secret made her dread the separation which now seemed very near.

For a week or two, Jo behaved so strangely that her sisters were quite bewildered. She rushed to the door when the postman rang. She was rude to Mr. Brooke whenever they met. And she sat looking at Meg with a sad face.

Two weeks after Jo's secret trip to town, Meg saw Laurie chasing Jo all over the garden. Shrieks of laughter were heard.

In a few minutes Jo bounced into the parlor. She laid herself on the sofa and pretended to read the newspaper.

"Anything interesting?" asked Meg.

"Nothing but a story," returned Jo.

"Read it aloud. That will keep you out of mischief," said Amy in her most grown-up tone.

"What's the name of the story?" asked Beth, wondering why Jo kept her face behind the paper.

"*The Rival Painters.*"

"That sounds well. Read it," said Meg.

Jo began to read very fast. The girls listened with interest, for the tale was romantic and somewhat sad. Most of the characters died.

"Who wrote it?" asked Beth, who had caught a glimpse of Jo's face.

The reader suddenly sat up, cast away the paper, and replied in a loud voice, "Your sister!"

"You?" cried Meg, dropping her work.

"It's very good," said Amy critically.

"I knew it! Oh, my Jo, I *am* so proud!" Beth ran to hug her sister.

How delighted they all were, to be sure! How Meg wouldn't believe it till she saw the words "Miss Josephine March" actually printed in the paper. How kindly Amy remarked on the artistic parts of the story. How Beth skipped and sang with joy. How proud Mrs. March was when she knew it. How Jo laughed, with tears in her eyes.

Jo told of her adventure to see the newspaper man. She explained how she had been waiting all this time to see if one of her stories would be printed. She added, "And when I went to get my answer, he said he liked them both. He doesn't pay beginners, only lets them print in his paper. So I let him have the two stories. I shall write more, and he's going to pay me for the next one. I *am* so happy, for I may be able to support myself and help the girls."

Jo's breath gave out. Wrapping her head in the paper, she shed a few tears. To earn her own money and earn the praise of those she loved were the dearest wishes of her heart. This seemed to be the first step toward that happy end.

# CHAPTER FOURTEEN

# *The Telegram*

"November is so dreary," grumbled Meg as she stood at the window one dull afternoon, looking out at the frostbitten garden. "And nothing pleasant *ever* happens here."

Beth sat at the other window. She said, "Two pleasant things are going to happen right away. Marmee is coming down the street. And Laurie is coming through the garden as if he had something nice to tell."

In they both came. Mrs. March asked her usual question, "Any letter from Father, girls?" And Laurie asked, "Won't some of you come for a drive?"

"Laurie, will you call at the post office?" asked Mrs. March as the girls went off for their coats. "It's our day for a letter."

A sharp ring of the door bell interrupted her. A minute later Hannah came in with a telegram.

Mrs. March read the two lines it contained and dropped back into her chair. It was as if the little paper had sent a bullet to her heart. Jo read aloud in a frightened voice:

*Mrs. March:*
*Your husband is very ill. Come at once.*
*S. Hale*
*Blank Hospital, Washington*

How still the room was as they listened. How strangely the day darkened. How suddenly the whole world seemed to change, as the girls gathered about their mother. They felt as if all the happiness and support of their lives was about to be taken from them.

Mrs. March stretched out her arms to her daughters. "I shall go at once," she said. "But it may be too late. Oh, children, help me to bear it!"

For several minutes there was nothing but the sound of sobbing in the room. They tried to be calm as their mother sat up. Looking pale but steady, she put away her grief to think and plan.

"Laurie, send a telegram saying I will come at once. The next train goes early in the morning. I'll take that. And please leave a note at Aunt March's. Jo, give me that pen and paper."

Jo knew what her mother was about to do. She would need money for the journey, and she must ask to borrow it from Aunt March. Her mother quickly made a list of errands, and Jo scurried out of the house.

Mr. Laurence hurried over to say how sad he was at the news. He offered to escort Mrs. March to Washington. Mrs. March thanked him kindly, but would not hear of that. Mr. Laurence marched off, saying he'd be back soon. No one thought of him again until Meg suddenly came upon Mr. Brooke in the door entry.

"I came to offer myself as escort to your mother," he said in a warm, quiet voice.

Meg put out her hand. "How kind you are! It will be such a relief to know she has someone to take care of her. Thank you very, very much!"

The short afternoon wore away. Jo had not been seen for hours, when at last she came walking in with a very odd expression. She handed a roll of money to her mother. "That's my part toward making Father comfortable and bringing him home!"

"Twenty-five dollars! Jo, I hope you haven't done anything rash."

"No, I only sold something that was my own."

As she spoke, Jo took off her bonnet. Everyone gasped, for her flowing hair was cut short.

"Your hair! Your beautiful hair!"

"Oh, Jo, how could you?"

"My dear girl, there was no need of this."

Jo rumpled her hair, trying to look as if she liked it. "It will do my brains good to have that mop taken off. My head feels so light and cool."

"What made you do it?" asked Amy, who would have cut off her head before cutting her pretty hair.

"Well, I was wild to do something for Father," replied Jo, as they gathered about the table. "I saw the barber shop and knew what I had to do. The woman there picked out a long lock for me to keep. I'll give it to you, Marmee."

Mrs. March put the wavy chestnut lock away with a short gray one in her desk. She only said, "Thank you, deary," but something in her face made the girls change the subject. They talked as cheerfully as they could about the happy times they would have when Father came home.

No one wanted to go to bed that evening. Finally Mrs. March put away her sewing and said, "Come girls." Beth went to the piano and played their father's favorite hymn. All began bravely, but broke down one by one till Beth was left alone, singing with all her heart.

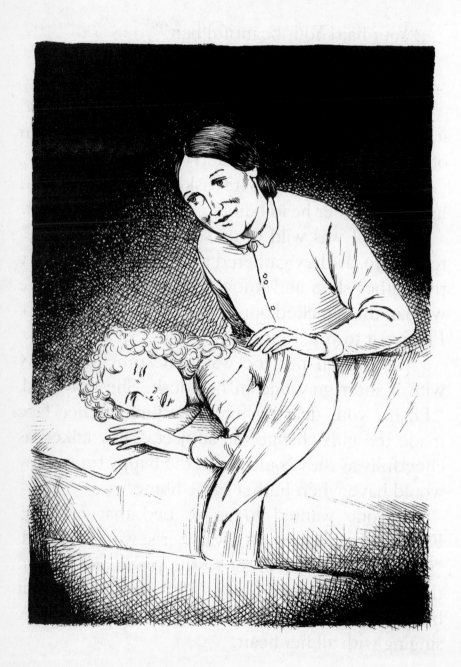

The clocks were striking midnight and the rooms were very still as a figure glided quietly from bed to bed. It smoothed a cover here and settled a pillow there, looking tenderly at each sleeping face. It kissed each, and prayed as only a mother can.

Mrs. March lifted the curtain. The moon came from behind the clouds and shone upon her like a kind face that seemed to whisper, "Be comforted, dear soul! There is always light behind the clouds."

As they dressed in the cold, gray dawn, the sisters agreed to say good-bye cheerfully and send their mother on her journey without tears.

The big trunk stood ready in the hall. Mother's cloak and bonnet lay on the sofa. Mother sat trying to eat, but looking pale and worn. Meg's eyes kept filling with tears. Jo hid her face more than once. The little girls wore troubled expressions.

As they waited for the carriage Mrs. March said to the girls, "Hope and keep busy. Visit the poor Hummels. Meg, watch over your sisters, and in any trouble go to Mr. Laurence. Be patient, Jo, and be my brave girl. Beth, comfort yourself with your music and help around the house. And you, Amy, help all you can, and keep happy, safe at home."

"We will, Mother! We will!"

The carriage approached with a rattle. That was the hardest minute. No one cried, though their hearts were very heavy. They kissed their mother quietly and clung about her tenderly.

Laurie and his grandfather came over to see her off. Mr. Brooke looked so strong and kind that the girls named him "Mr. Greatheart" on the spot.

"Good-bye, my darlings! God bless and keep us all!" whispered Mrs. March. She kissed one dear little face after the other, and hurried into the carriage. The girls tried to wave their hands cheerfully. As she rolled away, the sun came out. Looking back, she saw it shining on the group at the gate like a good sign.

# CHAPTER FIFTEEN

## *A Bitter Winter Wind*

For a week, everyone seemed in a heavenly frame of mind. Good news about their father comforted the girls very much. Mr. Brooke sent a letter every day, which grew more cheerful as the week passed. At first the girls were very well-behaved and serious. But as the news kept getting better, they began to fall back into their old ways.

Jo caught a bad cold and was ordered to stay at home till she was better. Amy grew bored with housework and returned to her art. Meg wrote long letters to her mother. Beth visited the Hummels and performed her little duties faithfully each day—and even some of her sisters'.

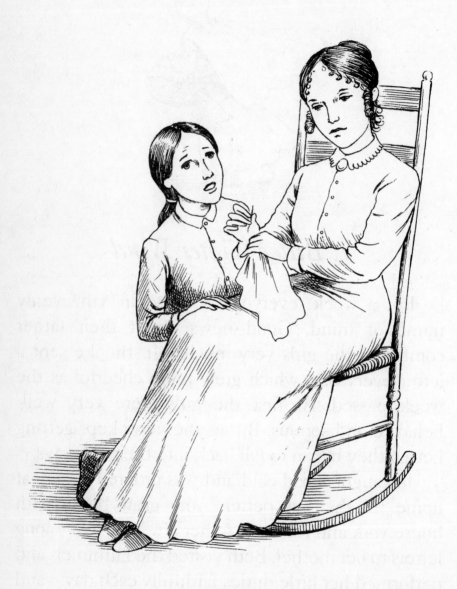

They all felt that they had done well and deserved praise. And so they did, but then they stopped doing well—and learned a hard lesson.

"Meg, I wish you'd go and see the Hummels. You know Mother told us not to forget them," said Beth. It had been ten days since Mrs. March had left.

"I'm too tired to go this afternoon," replied Meg, rocking comfortably.

"Can't you, Jo?" asked Beth.

"Too stormy for me with my cold," said Jo.

"Why don't you go yourself?" asked Meg.

"I have been every day. But the baby is sick, and I don't know what to do for it. It gets sicker and sicker. I think you or Hannah ought to go."

Meg promised she would go tomorrow.

So Beth quietly put on her hood, filled her basket with treats for the poor children, and went out into the chilly air. It was late when she came back. No one saw her creep upstairs and shut herself into her mother's room. Half an hour after, Jo found little Beth, looking very ill, her eyes red.

"What's the matter?" cried Jo.

Beth put out her hand as if to warn her off. She whispered quickly, "You've had the scarlet fever, haven't you, Jo?"

"Years ago, when Meg did. Why?"

"Oh, Jo, Mrs. Hummel's baby is dead! It died in my lap before she got home," cried Beth with a sob.

"My poor dear, how dreadful for you!" said Jo. She took her sister in her arms as she sat down.

"When I got there Mrs. Hummel had gone for a doctor. The baby seemed asleep, but all of a sudden if gave a little cry and trembled, and then lay very still. I knew it was dead."

"Don't cry, dear! What did you do?"

"I just sat and held it softly till Mrs. Hummel came with the doctor. He said it was dead, and that it was scarlet fever. He told me to go home and take medicine right away, or I'd have it."

"Oh, Beth, if you should be sick I never could forgive myself! What shall we do?" cried Jo with a frightened look. She hugged her close. "If Mother was only at home!" she said. "You've been with the baby every day for more than a week, so I'm afraid you are going to have it, Beth. I'll call Hannah. She knows all about sickness."

Hannah assured them that there was no need to worry. Everyone got scarlet fever, and if rightly treated, nobody died.

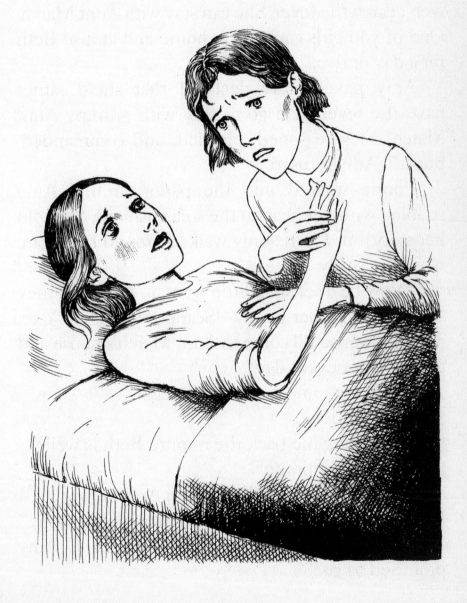

"We will have Dr. Bangs just take a look at you, dear," she said. "Then we'll send Amy off so she won't catch the fever. She can stay with Aunt March. One of you girls can stay at home and amuse Beth for a day or two."

Amy passionately declared that she'd rather have the fever than go to stay with grumpy Aunt March. Meg reasoned, pleaded, and commanded, but still Amy refused.

Laurie walked into the parlor to find Amy sobbing with her head in the sofa cushions. She told her story, but Laurie only walked around the room, whistling softly.

"Now be a sensible little woman, and do as they say," he urged her gently. "Scarlet fever is no joke, miss. I promise I'll come to Aunt March's house and take you out every day."

"Will you come every single day?"

"See if I don't."

"And bring me back the minute Beth is well?"

"The very minute."

"Well—I guess I will go," said Amy slowly.

"Good girl! Call Meg, and tell her you'll give in."

Meg and Jo came running down, and Amy promised to go.

"What a difficult world it is!" said Jo. "No sooner do we get out of one trouble than down comes another. I'm lost with Mother gone."

"I think we ought to tell her if Beth is really ill. But Hannah says Mother can't leave Father, and it will only make them anxious," worried Meg. "Jo, go and get Dr. Bangs at once. We can't decide anything till he has been."

Dr. Bangs came and said Beth had symptoms of the fever, but he thought she would have it lightly. Amy was ordered off to Aunt March's house.

# CHAPTER SIXTEEN

# *Dark Days*

Beth was much sicker than anyone imagined. Meg stayed at home so she would not infect the King children. She felt guilty when she wrote letters to Washington and did not tell anything about Beth's illness.

Jo devoted herself to Beth day and night. It was not a hard task, for Beth was a sweet and tender patient. But there came a time during the fever when she began to talk in a hoarse, broken voice. She played on the bed cover as if on her beloved little piano. She did not know the familiar faces around her, but called them by wrong names. She also called for her mother.

Jo grew frightened. Meg begged to write the truth. A letter from Washington added to their trouble. Mr. March had grown sicker and could not come home for a long while.

The days seemed dark now. The sisters were sad and lonely as they worked and waited, while the shadow of death hovered. Meg often sat alone with tears dropping on her work. She thought about how rich she had been in things more precious than anything money could buy—love, peace, and health. These were the real blessings of life.

Living in the darkened sick room, Jo learned to see the beauty and sweetness of Beth's nature. She felt how deep and tender a place she filled in all hearts. She realized the worth of Beth's goal to live for others and make home happy.

And Amy longed to be at home. She felt that no work would be troublesome. She grew sad as she remembered how many tasks Beth's willing hands had done for her.

Laurie haunted the house like a restless ghost. Mr. Laurence sadly locked the grand piano.

Everyone missed Beth. The milkman, baker, grocer, and butcher asked how she did. Neighbors sent all sorts of comforts and good wishes. Even the

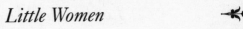

sisters were surprised to find how many friends Beth had made.

Dr. Bangs came twice a day. Hannah sat up at night. Meg kept a telegram in her desk ready to send off at any minute, and Jo never stirred from Beth's side.

The first of December, a bitter wind blew, snow fell fast, and the year seemed getting ready for its death. When Dr. Bangs came that morning, he looked long at Beth. He held her hot hand in his own, then laid it gently down.

"If Mrs. March can leave her husband she'd better be sent for," he said in a low voice.

Meg dropped down into a chair. Jo ran to the parlor, snatched up the telegram, and rushed out into the storm.

After Jo returned, Laurie came in with a letter from the post office saying that Mr. March was mending again. Jo's face was so full of misery that Laurie asked quickly, "Is Beth worse?"

"I've sent for Mother," said Jo.

"Oh, Jo, it's not so bad as that?" cried Laurie.

"Yes, it is. She doesn't know who we are. She doesn't look like my Beth, and there's nobody to help us bear it!"

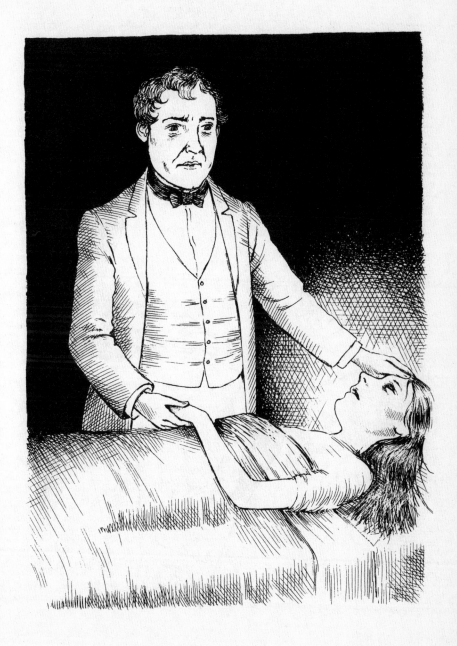

As the tears streamed down poor Jo's cheeks, she stretched out her hand. Laurie took it in his, whispering as well as he could with a lump in his throat, "I'm here. Hold on to me, Jo, dear!"

The warm grasp of his hand comforted Jo's sore heart. She cried miserably, and Laurie drew his hand across his eyes. As Jo's sobs quieted, he said hopefully, "I don't think she will die. She's so good, and we all love her so much. I don't believe God will take her away yet."

"The good and dear people always do die," groaned Jo. But she stopped crying, for her friend's words cheered her up in spite of her own doubts and fears.

"Poor girl, you're worn out. I'll hearten you up in a jiffy. Tonight I'll give you something that will warm your heart," said Laurie, beaming at her.

"What is it?" cried Jo.

"I secretly telegraphed your mother yesterday, and Brooke answered she'd come at once. She'll be here tonight, and everything will be all right. The late train is in at two in the morning."

Laurie spoke very fast and turned red and excited. Jo grew quite white and threw her arms round his neck, crying, "Oh, Laurie! I am so glad!"

Everyone rejoiced but Beth. She lay in a deep sleep. She woke only now and then to mutter, "Water!" All day Jo and Meg hovered over her, and all day the snow fell, the bitter wind raged, and the hours dragged slowly by.

Night came at last. The doctor had said that some change, for better or worse, would probably take place about midnight. Hannah lay down on the sofa. Mr. Laurence paced in the parlor. Laurie lay on the rug, staring into the fire.

The clock struck twelve, and Meg and Jo thought a change passed over Beth's face. An hour went by, and nothing happened except Laurie's quiet departure for the station. Another hour, still no one came. Fears of delay in the storm, or accidents—or, worst of all, a great grief in Washington—haunted the girls.

It was past two when Jo heard a movement by the bed. Turning quickly, she saw Meg kneeling before their mother's chair with her face hidden. A dreadful fear passed coldly over Jo as she thought, "Beth is dead, and Meg is afraid to tell me." A great change seemed to have taken place. The fever flush and the look of pain were gone, and the beloved little face looked peaceful.

Leaning low over her dearest sister, Jo kissed the damp forehead. She whispered softly, "Good-bye, my Beth. Good-bye!"

Hannah hurried to the bed. She looked at Beth, felt her hands, and listened at her lips. Then she exclaimed, "The fever's turned. Her skin's damp, and she breathes easy. Praise be given!"

"Yes, my dears, I think the little girl will pull through this time," said the doctor when he came.

"Listen!" cried Jo, jumping to her feet.

Yes, there was a sound of carriage bells at the door below, a cry from Hannah, and then Laurie's voice saying in a joyful whisper, "Girls, she's come! She's come!"

# CHAPTER SEVENTEEN

## *A Mother's Touch*

Words cannot describe the meeting of mother and daughters. The house filled with happiness. When Beth woke, the first thing she saw was her mother's face. She smiled and nestled close in the loving arms about her. Then she slept again. The girls waited upon their mother, for she would not unclasp the thin hand that clung to hers even in sleep.

Hannah served an astonishing breakfast, and Meg and Jo fed their mother like young storks. They listened to her whispered account of Father's health and Mr. Brooke's promise to stay with him. She told of the delays caused by the storm on the

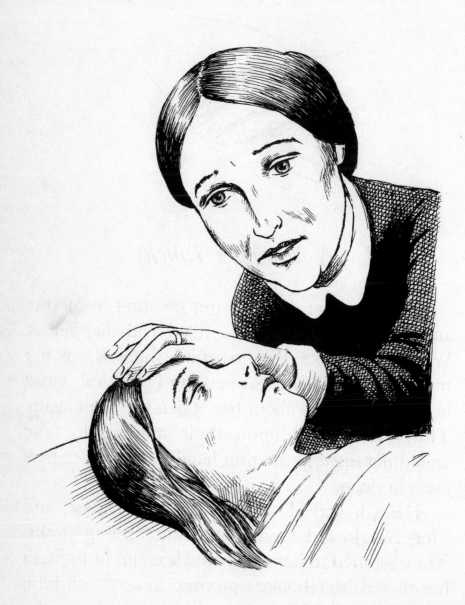

journey home, and the comfort Laurie's face had given her when she arrived at the station.

What a strange yet pleasant day that was. So brilliant and happy outside, for everyone seemed to be out welcoming the first snow. So quiet and restful inside, for everyone slept, and there was a stillness throughout the house. Mrs. March would not leave Beth's side. She rested in the big chair, waking often to look at and touch her child.

Laurie meanwhile set off for Aunt March's house to comfort Amy. Aunt March and Amy both had tears in their eyes when they heard the good news. By then, Laurie was tired from his long night, so Amy persuaded him to rest on the sofa.

Laurie was wakened later by Amy's cry of joy at the sight of her mother. There probably were a good many happy little girls in the city that day, but Amy was the happiest of all. She sat in her mother's lap and told her of her adventures with Aunt March and her pet parrot. Marmee saw something on Amy's hand that made her smile.

Amy said gravely, "Aunt gave me this turquoise ring today. She called me to her and kissed me, and put it on my finger, and said I was a credit to her. I'd like to wear it, Mother. Can I?"

"It's very pretty. But I think you're a little too young for such decorations, Amy," said Mrs. March. She looked down at the plump little hand with the band of sky-blue stones on the finger.

"I don't like it only because it's so pretty," said Amy. "I want to wear it to remind me of something. Beth isn't selfish, and that's the reason everyone loves her. I'm going to try and be like Beth all I can. If I had something always around me to remind me, I would do better. May we try this way?"

"Wear your ring, dear, and do your best. I think you will succeed, for the sincere wish to be good is half the battle. Now I must go back to Beth. Keep up your heart, little daughter, and we will soon have you home again."

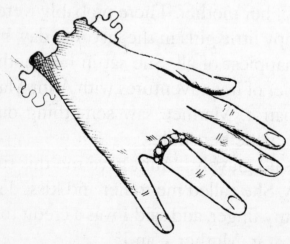

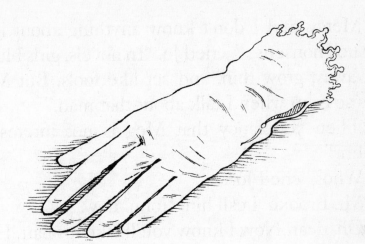

That evening Jo slipped upstairs into Beth's room. Marmee was in her usual place by the bed. Jo stood a minute, twisting her fingers in her hair with a worried look.

"What is it, deary?" asked Mrs. March, holding out her hand.

"I want to tell you something, Mother. Last summer Meg left a pair of gloves at the Laurences' and only one was returned. Now Laurie has told me that Mr. Brooke keeps it as a reminder of Meg. He said Mr. Brooke liked Meg but didn't dare say so, since she was so young and he so poor. Now, isn't it a dreadful state of things?"

"Do you think Meg cares for him?" asked Mrs. March.

"Mercy me! I don't know anything about love and such nonsense!" cried Jo. "In novels, girls blush, faint away, grow thin, and act like fools. But Meg looks so calm when I talk about that man."

"Then you fancy that Meg is not interested in John?"

"Who?" cried Jo.

"Mr. Brooke. I call him 'John' now."

"Oh, dear! Now I know you'll take his part. He's been good to Father, and you will let Meg marry him!" And Jo pulled her hair again angrily.

"My dear, don't get angry. I will tell you how it happened. John was so devoted to Father that we couldn't help getting fond of him. He told us he loves Meg. But he wants to have a comfortable home before he asks her to marry him. Besides, Meg *is* young, and I need to see for myself what *her* feelings are for *him*."

"She'll see those handsome eyes, and then it will be all up with her," Jo grumbled. "She likes brown eyes, and doesn't think John an ugly name, and she'll go and fall in love, and there's an end of peace and fun, and cozy times together. I see it all! Brooke will carry her off, and make a hole in the family, and break my heart. Why weren't we all boys? Then there wouldn't be any bother." Jo leaned her chin on her knees sadly.

Mrs. March said, "Jo, it is natural you should all go to homes of your own in time. But I do want to keep my girls as long as I can. Your father and I have agreed that Meg shall not be engaged nor married before twenty. If she and John love one another, they can wait."

"Wouldn't you rather have her marry a rich man?" asked Jo.

"I *would* like John to be firmly established in some good business before they are married. But I also know how much genuine happiness can be found in a plain little house."

"Well, I hate to see things going all crisscross and getting snarled up," said Jo. "I wish we could keep from growing up. But buds turn into roses, and kittens into cats!"

"What's that about cats?" asked Meg. She crept into the room with a letter to Father in her hand.

"Only one of my stupid speeches. I'm going to bed," said Jo.

Mrs. March glanced over Meg's letter to Father. "It's beautifully written. Please add that I send my love to John," said Mrs. March as she gave it back.

"Do you call him *John*?" asked Meg, smiling.

"Yes. He has been like a son to us, and we are very fond of him," replied Mrs. March. She looked carefully at her daughter.

"I'm glad of that, for he is so lonely. Good-night, Mother," said Meg.

The kiss her mother gave her was very tender. As she went away, Mrs. March said, "She does not know if she loves John yet, but will soon."

# CHAPTER EIGHTEEN

## *Father's Little Women*

The peaceful weeks that followed were like sunshine after a storm.

Mr. March began to write of returning early in the new year. Beth was soon able to lie on the study sofa all day. She was able to play with her cats and dolls. Jo took her for a daily walk around the house. Meg cheerfully burned her white hands cooking. Amy celebrated her return by giving away many of her treasures.

Several days of mild weather led to a wonderful Christmas Day. Mr. March wrote that he would soon be with them. And Beth felt especially well that morning.

"I'm so full of happiness. If Father was here, that would be the last drop I could hold," said Beth.

"So am I," added Jo.

"I'm sure I am," echoed Amy.

"Of course I am!" cried Meg.

Now and then things do happen like in a storybook. Half an hour after everyone had said they were so happy they could only hold one drop more, the drop came. Laurie opened the parlor door and popped his head in very quietly.

He might as well have turned a somersault and whooped. His face was so full of excitement that everyone jumped up. He said, "Here's another Christmas present for the March family."

In Laurie's place stood Mr. March, leaning on Mr. Brooke. He tried to say something and couldn't. Of course there was a stampede. For several minutes everybody seemed to lose their wits.

Mr. March became lost in the embrace of four pairs of loving arms. Jo nearly fainted. Mr. Brooke kissed Meg—entirely by mistake, of course. Amy tumbled over a stool, and hugged and cried over her father's boots. Mrs. March was the first to recover herself. She said, "Hush! Remember Beth."

But it was too late. The study door flew open. Beth ran straight into her father's arms. Then their full hearts overflowed.

There never was such a Christmas dinner as the one they had that day—a plump turkey, plum pudding and all the fixings. Mr. Laurence and his grandson dined with them, as well as Mr. Brooke. Jo frowned at this, which amused Laurie.

Beth and her father sat in two easy chairs at the head of the table. They drank toasts, told stories, sang songs, and had a very good time.

After the guests left, the happy family sat together round the fire. Mr. March took little Beth in his lap, looked with pride on his girls, and said, "I have discovered many things today."

"Oh, tell us what they are!" cried Meg.

"Here is one." He picked up Meg's hand. "I remember when this hand was white and smooth and you wanted to keep it that way. It was very pretty then, but to me it is much prettier now. You have a hard palm and pricked fingers from much work. And in these scars and scratches I see a little history. Meg, my dear, I'm proud to shake this good, hard-working little hand."

"What about Jo? Please say something nice. She has tried so hard and been so very, very good to me," said Beth in her father's ear.

He laughed and looked across at the tall girl. "In spite of the new short hair, I don't see the 'son Jo' whom I left a year ago," said Mr. March. "I see a young lady. Her face is rather thin and pale, but I like to look at it. It is gentler. She moves quietly, and takes care of a certain little sister in a motherly way that delights me. I rather miss my wild girl. But if I get a strong, helpful, sweet woman in her place, I shall feel quite satisfied."

"Now it's Beth's turn," said Amy, longing for her turn, but ready to wait.

"There's so little of her, I'm afraid to say much, for fear she will slip away altogether. Though she is not so shy as she used to be," began their father cheerfully. But remembering how nearly he *had* lost her, he held her close. "I've got you safe, my Beth. And I'll keep you so, please God."

He looked down at Amy, who sat at his feet, and said, "I saw that Amy ran errands for her mother all afternoon. She has waited on everyone with patience and good humor. She does not complain much. And she has not even mentioned a very pretty ring that she wears. She has learned to think of other people more and of herself less."

Beth perked up and smiled broadly.

"What are you thinking of, Beth?" asked Jo.

"It's singing time now, and I want to be in my old place," Beth said softly. "I have put music to the poem Father likes. It is the 'Song of the Shepherd Boy.' "

So, sitting at the dear little piano, Beth softly touched the keys. And in the sweet voice they had never thought they would hear again, she sang a lovely hymn.

# CHAPTER NINETEEN

## The Year Closes

Mother and daughters hovered around Mr. March the next day as he sat propped up in a big chair by Beth's sofa. Their happiness seemed complete. But something seemed to be "in the air."

Mr. and Mrs. March looked at one another nervously. They watched Meg, who was absent-minded, shy, and silent. She jumped whenever the bell rang, and blushed when John Brooke's name was mentioned.

Laurie came by in the afternoon. Seeing Meg at the window, he fell down on one knee in the snow, beat his chest, tore at his hair, and clasped his hands together.

"What does the goose mean by that?" said Meg, laughing.

"He's showing you how your John will act," answered Jo miserably.

"Don't say *my John*. It isn't proper or true. Jo, I've told you I don't care much about him. There isn't to be anything said."

"But something *has* been said. I see it, and so does Mother. You are not like your old self a bit, and seem ever so far away from me. I do wish it was all settled. If you mean to do it, have it over quickly," said Jo.

"I can't say anything till he speaks. And he won't, because Father said I was too young," began Meg. She smiled in a way that suggested she did not quite agree with her father.

"If he *did* speak, what would you say?"

"I've planned it all. I will calmly say, 'Thank you, Mr. Brooke. You are very kind, but I agree with Father that I am too young.'"

A sudden step in the hall made Meg fly into her chair and begin to sew as if her life depended on it.

"Good afternoon, Miss Jo. I came to get my umbrella—I mean, to see how your father is today," said Mr. Brooke nervously.

"It's very well, thank you. He's in the umbrella stand. I'll get him, and tell the umbrella you are here." And having jumbled her father and the umbrella together, Jo left the room to give Meg a chance to make her speech. But the instant Jo vanished, Meg murmured, "Mother will like to see you. I'll call her."

"Don't go. Are you afraid of me, Margaret?" John asked. Meg blushed up to the little curls on her forehead, for he had only called her *Miss* Margaret before. Then she put out her hand and said, "How can I be afraid when you have been so kind to Father? I only wish I could thank you for it."

"Shall I tell you how?" asked Mr. Brooke, looking at Meg with so much love that her heart began to flutter. "I only want to know if you care for me a little, Meg. I love you so much."

This was the moment for her speech, but Meg forgot every word of it and answered, "I don't know."

He pressed her hand gratefully, and said, "Will you try and find out? I want to know so much."

Just at that moment, Aunt March came hobbling in. Mr. Brooke vanished into the study.

"Bless me, what's all this?" cried the old lady.

"It's Father's friend. I'm so surprised to see you!" stammered Meg.

"What is Father's friend saying to make you blush so?" returned Aunt March, sitting down.

"Mr. Brooke came for his umbrella," began Meg.

"Brooke? That boy's tutor? Ah! I understand now," cried Aunt March, looking shocked. "Do you mean to marry this man? If you do, not one penny of my money ever goes to you."

Now, if Aunt March had begged Meg to *accept* John Brooke, Meg probably would have declared she couldn't *think* of it. But when ordered *not* to like him, Meg immediately made up her mind that she would.

"I shall marry whom I please, Aunt March. You can leave your money to anyone you like!"

"Now, Meg, my dear, you ought to marry rich to help your family. I thought you had more sense."

"John is good and wise. He's got heaps of talent, he's willing to work, and he's so brave," said Meg.

"He knows you have rich relatives, child. That's why he likes you."

"Aunt March, how dare you say such a thing? My John wouldn't marry for money, any more than I would. I'm not afraid of being poor."

"Well, I wash my hands of the whole affair! Don't expect anything from me when you are married. I'm done with you forever."

Slamming the door in Meg's face, Aunt March left. Meg did not know whether to laugh or cry. Before she could make up her mind, she was embraced by Mr. Brooke.

"I couldn't help hearing, Meg. Thank you for defending me. You do care for me a little bit."

"I didn't know how much till Aunt March said those things about you," began Meg.

"May I stay and be happy, dear?"

"Yes, John," said Meg.

Fifteen minutes later, Jo came softly downstairs. At the door she saw something that stopped her. Her mouth was nearly as wide open as her eyes. There was Mr. Brooke, the enemy, sitting on the sofa with Meg upon his knee!

Jo gave a sort of gasp. Mr. Brooke laughed and said, "Sister Jo, congratulate us!"

Jo vanished without a word. She cried as she told the awful news to Beth and Amy. The little girls, however, thought it was a wonderful event, and Jo got little comfort from them.

Mr. and Mrs. March went into the parlor to talk with the happy couple. Mr. Brooke asked for Meg's hand in marriage, and they agreed to a wedding in three years, when Meg would be twenty.

Mr. Brooke proudly took Meg into supper that evening. They both looked so happy that Jo didn't have the heart to be jealous. No one ate much, but everyone looked very happy. The old room seemed to brighten up amazingly when the first romance of the family began there.

"You can't say nothing pleasant ever happens now, can you, Meg?" said Amy.

"No, I'm sure I can't. So much has happened since I said that!" answered Meg.

Mrs. March said, "This has been a year full of events, but it ends well, after all."

Old Mr. Laurence and his grandson came by. Laurie came prancing in bearing a great bridal-looking bouquet. He was invited to the wedding on the spot.

"I'll come if I'm at the ends of the earth, for the sight of Jo's face would alone be worth a long journey. Jo, what's the matter?" asked Laurie, following her into a corner of the parlor.

"You can't know how hard it is for me to give up Meg. I've lost my dearest friend."

"You've got me, anyhow. I'll stand by you all the days of my life." And Laurie meant what he said. "Don't be sad. Meg is happy. I shall be through college before long, and then we'll go to Europe on some nice trip."

"There's no knowing what may happen in three years," said Jo.

"That's true. Don't you wish you could see where we shall all be then? I do," returned Laurie.

Jo's eyes went slowly round the room, brightening as they looked. Father and Mother sat together, quietly reliving a romance which began some twenty years ago. Amy was drawing the lovebirds, who sat apart in a beautiful world of their own. Beth lay on her sofa, talking cheerily with old Mr. Laurence. Jo lounged in her favorite seat. Laurie, leaning on the back of her chair, smiled at her in the long mirror which reflected them both.

"I think not, for I might see something sad," said Jo. "Everyone looks so happy now. I don't believe they could be much improved."

And so the curtain falls—for now—upon Meg, Jo, Beth, and Amy in this first act of the story called *Little Women*.

The End of Part I — *Little Women*

Part II — *Good Wives*

## LOUISA MAY ALCOTT

Louisa May Alcott was born in 1832 in Concord, Massachusetts. Her father was a brilliant thinker with famous writer friends, but he earned little money. In her teenage years, young Louisa helped to support her family. She was a schoolteacher and nurse, she took in sewing and laundry, and she worked as a maid. She also found time to write—stories, poems and plays—and published her first pieces when she was twenty-one.

For several years, Alcott supported her family by writing "thriller" or "romantic" stories. Then a publisher requested a book for girls, so Alcott wrote *Little Women*, using her own life with her four sisters as inspiration. (She put herself in the story—as Jo March.) The book was published in 1868. It became an immediate success, and remains a favorite classic to this day. Part Two was published in 1869 as *Good Wives*, and the two parts were reissued as a single book in 1871.

Alcott wrote several more books about the March family, including *Little Men* (1871), and *Jo's Boys* (1886). She also worked for women's rights. Alcott died in Boston in 1888.

# POLLYANNA

ELEANOR H. PORTER

CONDENSED AND ADAPTED BY
LAURA HILL

ILLUSTRATED BY
JON SAYER

COVER ILLUSTRATED BY
JERRY DILLINGHAM

# CONTENTS

Characters.................................................. 192

1. Miss Polly............................................... 197

2. The Little Attic Room .......................... 209

3. The Game ............................................. 221

4. Pollyanna Goes Visiting ....................... 233

5. Pollyanna to the Rescue ....................... 249

6. Just a Matter of Jelly............................ 265

7. A Red Rose and a Lace Shawl ............... 275

8. "A Mystery".......................................... 283

9. Prisms ................................................. 293

10. Surprises.............................................. 301

11. And More Surprises.............................. 307

12. The Accident........................................ 319

13. A Woman's Hand and Heart................. 327

14. A Child's Presence .............................. 341

15. The Game and Its Players .................... 349

16. Through an Open Window.................... 361

17. A Letter from Pollyanna ...................... 374

About the Author.................................. 377

POLLYANNA WHITTIER — a lonely but cheerful eleven-year-old orphan girl who comes to live with her spinster Aunt Polly

MISS POLLY HARRINGTON (AUNT POLLY) — the stern older sister of Pollyanna's mother, not at all sure she's ready to care for a child

NANCY — Aunt Polly's hard-working housemaid, and Pollyanna's soft-hearted friend

JOHN PENDLETON — a crabby, mysterious neighbor who finds he needs Pollyanna

DR. THOMAS CHILTON — a kindly doctor who changes Pollyanna's life in several ways

# CHARACTERS

**MRS. SNOW** — an invalid neighbor lady who learns from Pollyanna the importance of being glad

**MILLY** — Mrs. Snow's daughter

**OLD TOM** — Aunt Polly's gardener

**JIMMY BEAN** — a little boy who finds a friend in a fellow orphan

**DR. WARREN** — the doctor who is called to attend to Pollyanna

**WIDOW TARBELL** AND **MRS. BENTON** — two of the many visitors who express well wishes for Pollyanna

# *Pollyanna*

# CHAPTER ONE

## *Miss Polly*

Miss Polly Harrington entered her kitchen a little hurriedly this June morning. Miss Polly did not usually hurry. She prided herself on her calm manner. But today she was actually hurrying.

Nancy, washing dishes at the sink, looked up in surprise. Nancy had been working in Miss Polly's kitchen only two months, but already she knew that her mistress did not usually hurry.

"Nancy!" Miss Polly called sternly.

"Yes, ma'am," Nancy answered cheerfully, wiping a pitcher in her hand.

"Nancy, when I'm talking to you, please stop your work and listen to what I have to say."

Nancy's face flushed. She set the pitcher down and nearly tipped it over, which made her even more nervous.

"Yes, ma'am, I will, ma'am," she stammered. "I was only keepin' on with my work 'cause you specially told me to hurry with my dishes."

Her mistress frowned.

"That will do, Nancy. I did not ask for explanations," Miss Polly said. "When you've finished, you may clear the little room at the head of the stairs in the attic, and make up the bed. Sweep the room and clean it, of course, after you clear out the trunks and boxes."

Miss Polly paused, then went on. "I suppose I may as well tell you now, Nancy. My niece, Miss Pollyanna Whittier, is coming to live with me. She is eleven years old, and will sleep in that room."

"A little girl—coming here, Miss Harrington? Oh, won't that be nice!" cried Nancy.

"Nice? Well, that isn't exactly the word I would use," said Miss Polly stiffly. "However, I intend to make the best of it. I am a good woman, and I know my duty. See that you clean the corners, Nancy," she finished sharply, as she left the room.

"Yes, ma'am," sighed Nancy.

In her own room, Miss Polly took out the letter she had received days before from a faraway Western town. It had been an unpleasant surprise to her. The letter was addressed to Miss Polly Harrington, Beldingsville, Vermont. It read:

*Dear Madam:*

*I regret to inform you that the Rev. John Whittier died two weeks ago, leaving one child, a girl eleven years old. He left practically nothing else for the child except a few books. As you doubtless know, he was the pastor of this small mission church, and had a very small salary.*

*He had expressed that for your sister's sake you might wish to bring the child up with her own family in the East. If you can take her, we would appreciate it very much if you would telegram at once. A man and his wife here are going East very soon. They would take her with them to Boston and put her on the Beldingsville train. Of course you would be notified when to expect Pollyanna.*

*Hoping to hear from you soon, I remain,*
*Respectfully yours,*
*Jeremiah O. White.*

With a frown, Miss Polly folded the letter and tucked it into its envelope. She had telegrammed saying she would take the child, of course. She *hoped* she knew her duty well enough for that!

As she sat, she thought about her older sister, Jennie, the child's mother. Jennie, as a girl of twenty, had insisted upon marrying the young minister. Her family had hoped she would marry another man who also loved her—a richer, older man. But Jennie loved the minister. So she married him and moved away to become a missionary.

Polly had been only fifteen when her sister moved away. The family had little more to do with Jennie. Jennie had written, for a time. She named her last baby "Pollyanna" for her two sisters, Polly and Anna. The other babies had all died. A few years after the child's birth, the minister wrote a little heartbroken note, telling them of Jennie's death.

"I'm glad I know my duty," thought Miss Polly as she climbed the stairs to the attic room. "But *Pollyanna*! What a ridiculous name!"

The room contained a small bed, neatly made, two straight-backed chairs, a washstand, a dresser with no mirror, and a small table. No curtains. No pictures. All day the sun had been pouring down, and the little room was like an oven. There were no screens on the closed windows. A big fly was buzzing angrily at a window, trying to get out.

"Nancy," Miss Polly said later downstairs, "I found a fly in Miss Pollyanna's room. I have ordered screens, but until they come I expect you to see that the windows remain closed. My niece will arrive tomorrow at four o'clock. Please meet her at the station. The telegram says 'light hair, red-checked gingham dress, and straw hat.' "

Promptly at twenty minutes to four the next afternoon, Timothy the handyman and Nancy drove off to meet the expected guest.

And there she stood at the station—a slender little girl in a red-checked gingham with two fat braids of golden hair hanging down her back. Beneath the straw hat, an eager, freckled little face turned right and left, plainly searching for someone. She was standing by herself when Nancy approached her.

"Are you Miss—Pollyanna?" Nancy asked. The next moment she found herself half smothered in two gingham-clad arms.

"Oh, I'm so glad, *glad*, GLAD to see you," cried an eager voice. "Of course I'm Pollyanna, and I'm so glad you came to meet me! I hoped you would."

"You—you did?" stammered Nancy, wondering how Pollyanna could possibly have known her.

"Oh, yes. I've been wondering all the way here what you looked like," cried the little girl, dancing on her toes. "And now I know, and I'm glad you look just like you do."

Pollyanna's words were very confusing to Nancy. She was relieved when Timothy came up and the three were off at last. Nancy was dazed by all the little girl's comments and questions.

"Is it far? I hope it is—I love to ride," sighed Pollyanna. "Of course, if it isn't far I won't mind, 'cause I'll be glad to get there all the sooner. What a pretty street! I *knew* it was going to be pretty. Father told me…" The girl paused, with tears in her eyes. Then she went on. "Oh, I ought to explain about this red gingham dress, you know, and why I'm not in black. Part of the Ladies' Aid wanted to buy me a black dress and hat, but the other part thought the money ought to go toward the red carpet for the church, you know."

Pollyanna paused for breath, and Nancy stammered, "Well—I'm sure it'll be all right."

"I'm *glad* you feel that way. I do, too," nodded Pollyanna, again with a choking little breath. "Of course, 'twould have been a good deal harder to be glad in black—"

"Glad?" gasped Nancy.

"Yes—that Father's gone to Heaven to be with Mother. He said I *must* be glad. It's been pretty hard to do it, even in red gingham. But now it'll be easier because I've got you, Aunt Polly. I'm so glad I've got you!"

"Oh, but you've made an awful mistake, d-dear," Nancy said. "I'm only Nancy. I ain't your Aunt Polly, at all!"

"You—you *aren't*?" said the little girl in dismay.

"I'm Nancy, the hired girl. I do all the work except the washin' an' hard ironin'."

"But there *is* an Aunt Polly?" demanded the child anxiously. "You know she's all the aunt I've got. Father told me she lived in a lovely, great big house way on top of a hill."

"She does. You can see it now, you can," said Nancy. "It's that big white one with the green blinds, way ahead."

# CHAPTER TWO

## *The Little Attic Room*

Miss Polly Harrington looked up from her book as Nancy and the little girl appeared in the doorway. Miss Polly coldly held out a hand.

"How do you do, Pollyanna? I—" She had no chance to say more. Pollyanna had flown across the room and flung herself into her aunt's lap.

"Oh, Aunt Polly, Aunt Polly, I don't know how to be glad enough that you let me come to live with you," she was sobbing. "You don't know how perfectly lovely it is to have you and Nancy and all this after I've had just the Ladies' Aid!"

"Yes, well," said Miss Polly, trying to unclasp the girl. "You had a trunk, I presume?"

"Oh, yes, indeed, Aunt Polly. I've got a beautiful trunk that the Ladies' Aid gave me. I haven't got much in it—of my own, I mean. There were all Father's books. You see, Father—"

"Pollyanna," interrupted her aunt sharply, "there is one thing you should understand right away. I do not wish to have you talking about your father to me."

The little girl drew in her breath timidly.

"We will go upstairs to your room. You may follow me, Pollyanna."

Pollyanna turned quietly and followed her aunt from the room. Her eyes were brimming with tears, but her chin was bravely high.

"After all, I reckon I'm glad she doesn't want me to talk about Father," Pollyanna thought. "It'll be easier, maybe, if I don't talk about him. Probably that is why she told me not to—out of—kindness to me." And Pollyanna blinked off the tears and looked happily about her.

Pollyanna's small feet pattered behind her aunt. Her big blue eyes took in all the beautiful furniture, carpets, and pictures. She didn't want to miss anything in this wonderful house. Which door led to the room that was to be her very own?

Would it be beautiful and full of lace curtains, rugs, and pictures? Her aunt opened a door… but it only led to another stairway—a dreary stairway with bare walls on either side. At the top of the stairs were low, shadowy halls and corners stacked with trunks and boxes. Then she saw that her aunt had thrown open a door at the right.

"Pollyanna, here is your room, and your trunk is here, I see. Do you have your trunk key?"

Pollyanna nodded. Her eyes were a little wide and frightened.

Her aunt frowned.

"When I ask a question, Pollyanna, I prefer that you answer aloud, not merely with your head."

"Yes, Aunt Polly."

"Thank you. That is better. I believe you have everything that you need here," she added. "I will send Nancy up to help you unpack. Supper is at six o'clock." She left the room briskly.

For a moment Pollyanna stood quite still, looking after her. Then she turned her wide eyes to the bare wall, the bare floor, the bare windows. She turned them last to the little trunk and stumbled blindly toward it. She fell on her knees at its side, covering her face with her hands.

Nancy found her there when she came up a few minutes later.

"There, there, you poor lamb," Nancy crooned, hugging the little girl. "I was just a-fearin' I'd find you like this. Come, we'll get inside this trunk and take out your dresses in no time."

Nancy's quick hands unpacked the books, the patched underclothes, and the few pitiful dresses. Pollyanna, smiling bravely now, flew about, hanging the dresses in the closet. She stacked the books on the table and put away the underclothes in the dresser drawers.

"I'm sure it's going to be a very nice room. Don't you think so?" the girl stammered, after a while. "And I can be glad there isn't any looking glass here, for then I can't see my freckles."

At one of the windows, Pollyanna gave a glad cry and clapped her hands joyously.

"Oh, Nancy, I hadn't seen this before," she breathed. "Look 'way off there, with those trees and the houses and that lovely church spire, and the river shining just like silver. Why, Nancy, nobody needs any pictures on the wall with *that* to look at. Oh, I'm so *glad* now she let me have this room!"

"If you ain't a little angel from Heaven," cried Nancy. "Oh, land! There's her bell!" Nancy sprang to her feet and dashed out of the room.

Left alone, Pollyanna went back to her "picture." After a time she touched the window sash slowly... It was *so* hot in the room... To her joy the sash moved, and the next moment the window was wide open! Pollyanna leaned far out, drinking in the fresh, sweet air. A huge tree flung its branches against the window, like outstretched arms, inviting her. Suddenly she laughed aloud.

The next moment she had climbed to the window ledge. From there it was easy to step to the nearest tree branch. Clinging like a monkey, she swung herself from limb to limb until she reached the lowest branch. The drop to the ground was a little fearsome, but she landed on all fours, picked herself up, and looked eagerly about.

She was at the back of the house. Before her lay a garden where a bent old man was working. Beyond the garden a little path led up a steep hill. At the top, a lone pine tree stood beside a huge rock. To Pollyanna, at the moment, there seemed to be just one place in the world worth being—the top of that big rock.

With a run, Pollyanna skipped by the bent old man, and made her way between the rows of green growing things. A little out of breath, she reached the path, then began to climb. Already, however, she was thinking what a long way off that rock must be. Back at the window it had looked so near!

Fifteen minutes later the great clock in the hallway of the Harrington home struck six. At the last stroke Nancy sounded the bell for supper.

One, two, three minutes passed. Miss Polly frowned and tapped the floor with her shoe. She rose to her feet, went into the hall, and looked upstairs. She listened for a minute, then turned and swept into the dining room.

"Nancy," she said, as soon as the serving-maid appeared, "my niece is late. You need not call her. I told her what time supper was, and now she will have to suffer the consequences. When she comes down she may have bread and milk in the kitchen."

After supper, Nancy crept up the back stairs to the attic room.

"Bread and milk, indeed, when the poor lamb has only just cried herself to sleep," she muttered. She softly pushed open the door. The next moment she gave a frightened cry. "Where are you? Where've you gone? Where *have* you gone?" she panted. She looked in the closet, under the bed, and even in the trunk and down the water pitcher. Then she flew downstairs and out to Old Tom, the gardener.

"Mr. Tom, Mr. Tom, that blessed child's gone," she wailed. "She's vanished right up into Heaven where she come from, poor lamb!"

The old man straightened up.

"Gone? Heaven? Well, Nancy, it do look like as if she'd tried to get to Heaven," he agreed. He pointed with a crooked finger to where a slender figure was poised on top of a huge rock.

# CHAPTER THREE

## *The Game*

"For land's sake, Miss Pollyanna, what a scare you did give me," panted Nancy. She hurried up to the big rock as Pollyanna slid down.

"I didn't even know you'd went," cried Nancy, tucking the little girl's hand under her arm and hurrying her down the hill. "Poor little lamb! And you must be hungry, too. I'm afraid you'll have to have bread and milk in the kitchen with me, because you didn't come down to supper."

"But I couldn't. I was up here."

"Yes, but—she didn't know that, you see!" chuckled Nancy. "I'm sorry about the bread and milk, I am, I am."

"Oh, I'm not. I'm glad."

"Glad? Why?"

"Why, I like bread and milk, and I'd like to eat with you. I don't see any trouble about being glad about that."

"You don't seem to see any trouble bein' glad about everythin'," replied Nancy.

Pollyanna laughed softly. "Well, that's the game, you know, anyway."

"The—*game*?"

"Yes, the 'just being glad' game. Father told it to me, and it's lovely," said Pollyanna. "We've played it always, ever since I was a little, little girl. We began it when some crutches came in a missionary barrel."

"*Crutches!*"

"Yes. You see, I'd wanted a doll. But when the barrel came the lady wrote that no dolls came in, just the little crutches. So she sent 'em along. The game was to find something about everything to be glad about, no matter what," said Pollyanna. "We began right then—on the crutches."

"Well, goodness me! I can't see anythin' to be glad about—gettin' a pair of crutches when you wanted a doll."

"There is—there is," Pollyanna crowed. "*I* couldn't see it, either, Nancy, at first. Father had to tell it to me. You just be glad because you *don't—need—'em!* You see, it's easy when you know how! Only sometimes it's almost too hard, like when your father goes to Heaven."

"Yes, or when you're put in a snippy little room 'way at the top of the house with nothin' in it," growled Nancy.

Pollyanna sighed. "That was a hard one, at first, 'specially when I was so lonesome and I *had* been wanting pretty things! Then I saw that lovely picture out the window, so I knew I'd found things to be glad about. You see, when you're hunting for the glad things, you sort of forget the other kind. I suppose, though, it'll be a little harder now, since I haven't anybody to play the game with..." Then she added brightly, "Maybe Aunt Polly will play it, though!"

"My stars and stockings!—*Her?*" Nancy said to herself. Aloud she said, "Pollyanna, I ain't sayin' that I'll play it very well, but I'll play the game with ye, somehow—I just will, I will!"

"Oh, Nancy," cried Pollyanna, giving her a hug. "That'll be splendid! We'll have such fun!"

Pollyanna ate her bread and milk cheerfully. Then she went into the sitting room, where her aunt sat reading. Miss Polly looked up coldly.

"Have you had your supper, Pollyanna?"

"Yes, Aunt Polly."

"I'm very sorry, Pollyanna, that I had to send you into the kitchen to eat bread and milk."

"But I was real glad you did it, Aunt Polly. I like bread and milk, and Nancy, too. You mustn't feel bad about that one bit."

Aunt Polly sat suddenly a little more straight in her chair.

"Pollyanna, it's quite time you were in bed. You have had a hard day. Tomorrow we must plan your hours and see what new clothes you might need. Nancy will give you a candle. Breakfast will be at half-past seven. See that you are on time. Good night."

Pollyanna came straight to her aunt's side and gave her a loving hug. "I've had such a beautiful time, so far," she sighed happily. "I know I'm going to just love living with you. Good night," she called cheerfully, as she ran from the room.

"Well, upon my soul!" exclaimed Miss Polly. "What an extraordinary child."

Fifteen minutes later, in the attic room, a lonely little girl sobbed into the tightly-clutched sheet.

"I know, Father-among-the-angels, I'm not playing the game one bit now—not one bit. But I don't believe even you could find anything to be glad about sleeping all alone 'way off up here in the dark—like this. If only I was near Nancy or even Aunt Polly, it would be easier!"

It was nearly seven o'clock when Pollyanna awoke the next day. The air blew in fresh and sweet. The birds were twittering joyously, and Pollyanna flew to the window to talk to them. There, below her window, was Aunt Polly among the rosebushes. Pollyanna quickly dressed and sped down the stairs, leaving both doors open.

"Oh, Aunt Polly!" she called out. "I reckon I am glad this morning just to be alive!"

But Aunt Polly was not glad when she found flies buzzing about at breakfast. Nor was she glad that they had come in through the attic windows! Heat or no heat, the windows were to be shut!

Pollyanna's patched and worn-out clothes were also a disappointment.

"Pollyanna, we will drive to town at half-past one this afternoon," Aunt Polly said. "Not one of these things is fit for my niece to wear. You'll enter school in the fall. Meanwhile, I wish to hear you read aloud half an hour each day."

"I love to read," cried the girl. "I like to read to myself, on account of the big words, you know."

"It is also my duty to see that you are properly instructed in music," went on Aunt Polly. "I shall teach you sewing myself, of course. And you shall learn how to cook…" She paused, then went on slowly. "At nine o'clock every morning you will read aloud to me. Before that you will put this room in order. Wednesday and Saturday after half-past nine, you will spend with Nancy in the kitchen, learning to cook. Other mornings you will sew with me. That leaves afternoons for your music," she finished, and arose from her chair.

Pollyanna cried out in dismay, "Oh, but Aunt Polly, Aunt Polly, you haven't left me any time at all just to live! I'd be *breathing* all the time I was doing those things, but I wouldn't be living. Playing outdoors, reading, climbing hills, talking to Nancy. That's what I call living, Aunt Polly."

"Pollyanna! You will be allowed a proper amount of playtime, of course. But if I am willing to see that you have proper care and instruction, *you* must see that they are not wasted."

"Oh, Aunt Polly, as if I ever could be ungrateful. Why, *I love you!*"

"Yes, well, I *will* do my duty by you," said Miss Polly. She turned toward the door.

Indeed, Miss Polly *did* do her duty by her in many respects. She did take her to town for new church dresses and school clothes. She did sign her up for school in the fall. She fed her promptly three times a day, and allowed for playtime.

What Miss Polly did *not* offer—what her heart could not offer—Pollyanna found in other ways. With Nancy she played the "glad game," and talked about her father. With the family gardener, Old Tom, she talked of her mother. He would sit and tell her all he remembered about "Miss Jennie." And in the birds and the flowers and the outdoors, she found comfort.

When Miss Polly found the little girl sleeping out under the stars on the flat roof of the sunroom, she *finally* did her duty and moved her out of the hot attic room. Pollyanna was moved to the room below—and she was delighted to find it also had a lovely "picture window."

# CHAPTER FOUR

## *Pollyanna Goes Visiting*

It was not long before life at the Harrington home settled into order. Pollyanna sewed, practiced music, read aloud, and studied cooking, it is true. But she did not spend as much time on these as her aunt had planned.

She had more time to "just live." Almost every afternoon from two until six o'clock was hers to do with as she liked. There were no children in the neighborhood for Pollyanna to play with. The house itself was on the outskirts of the village. But she told Nancy, "I'm happy just to walk around and see the streets and the houses and watch the people. I just love people. Don't you?"

Almost every pleasant afternoon Pollyanna begged for an errand to run, so that she might be off for a walk. It was on these walks that she often met "the Man." The Man wore a long black coat and a high silk hat. His face was clean-shaven and rather pale and his hair was somewhat gray. He walked stiffly, and rather rapidly, and he was always alone. Pollyanna felt a little sorry for him. Perhaps that is why she spoke to him one day.

"How do you do, sir? Isn't this a nice day?" she called cheerily as she approached him.

The man stopped uncertainly.

"Did you speak—to me?" he asked sharply.

"Yes, sir," she beamed. "It's a nice day, isn't it?"

"Eh? Oh! Humph!" he grunted, and strode off. Pollyanna laughed. He was such a funny man.

The next day she saw him again.

"It isn't quite so nice as yesterday, but it's pretty nice," she called out cheerfully.

"Eh? Oh! Humph!" grunted the man, and once again Pollyanna laughed.

When for the third time Pollyanna talked to him, the man stopped.

"See here, child, who are you, and why are you speaking to me every day?"

"I'm Pollyanna Whittier, and I thought you looked lonesome. I'm so glad you stopped. Now we've met—only I don't know your name yet."

"Well, of all the—" The man did not finish his sentence, but strode on faster than ever.

Pollyanna looked after him. "But that was only half an introduction. I don't know *his* name, yet," she murmured, and went on her way.

Pollyanna was carrying calf's-foot jelly to Mrs. Snow today. Miss Polly sent something to Mrs. Snow once a week, since Mrs. Snow was poor, sick, and a member of her church. Today Pollyanna had begged to go, and Miss Polly had allowed it.

Pollyanna knocked on the door of the shabby little cottage. A pale, tired-looking girl answered.

"How do you do?" began Pollyanna politely. "I'm from Miss Polly Harrington, and I'd like to see Mrs. Snow, please."

"I'm Milly, her daughter. Please follow me."

In the sickroom, Pollyanna blinked a little in the gloom. Then she saw a woman half-sitting up in the bed across the room.

"How do you do, Mrs. Snow? Aunt Polly says she hopes you are comfortable today. She's sent you some calf's-foot jelly."

"Dear me," said a fretful voice. "And I was hoping for lamb broth today."

The sick woman pulled herself up till she sat up in the bed. It was a most unusual thing for her to do, though Pollyanna did not know this.

"I'm Pollyanna Whittier. I'm Miss Polly Harrington's niece, and I've come to live with her. That's why I'm here this morning."

"Very well, thank you. Your aunt is very kind, of course. But my appetite isn't very good this morning." She stopped suddenly, then went on, "I never slept a wink last night—not a wink!"

"Oh, dear, I wish *I* didn't," sighed Pollyanna. "You lose such a lot of time just sleeping! Don't you think so?"

"Lose time—sleeping?" exclaimed the woman.

"Yes, when you might be just living, you know. It seems such a pity we can't live nights, too."

The woman pulled herself higher up in bed.

"Well, if you ain't an amazing young one!" she cried. "Go to that window and pull up the curtain. I would like to know what you look like!"

"Oh, dear! Then you'll see my freckles, won't you?" Pollyanna sighed and went to the window. "There!" she said, as she turned back to the bed. "I'm so glad you wanted to see me, for now I can see you! They didn't tell me you were so pretty!"

"Me!—pretty?" scoffed the woman.

"Your eyes are so big and dark, and your hair's dark, too, and curly," cooed Pollyanna. "Why, Mrs. Snow, you *are* pretty! Just let me show you!"

Pollyanna skipped over to the dresser and picked up a small mirror.

"If you don't mind, I'd like to fix your hair just a little before I let you see it. May I, please?"

For five minutes Pollyanna worked swiftly. Meanwhile, the sick woman was beginning to feel excited in spite of herself.

"There!" panted Pollyanna, plucking a pink flower from a vase nearby and tucking it into the dark hair. She held out the mirror.

"Humph!" grunted the sick woman, eyeing her reflection. "I like red flowers better than pink ones. But then they fade anyhow before night, so what's the difference?"

"But you should be glad they fade! Then you can get more! And then I could fix your hair again. I love your black hair. It shows up so much nicer on a pillow than yellow hair does! I would be so glad if I only had it," sighed Pollyanna.

Mrs. Snow let the mirror drop.

"Well, you wouldn't if you were me. You wouldn't be glad for black hair nor anything else, if you had to lie here all day as I do!"

Pollyanna frowned. "It would be kind of hard to be glad about things, wouldn't it?" she said.

"Be glad about things—when you're sick in bed? I should say it would," replied Mrs. Snow.

"Tell me something to be glad about!"

To Mrs. Snow's amazement, Pollyanna sprang to her feet and clapped her hands.

"Oh, goody! That'll be a hard one—won't it? I've got to go, now, but I'll think and think all the way home. Good-bye. I've had a lovely time!" she called, as she tripped through the doorway.

"Well, I never! Now, what does she mean by that?" exclaimed Mrs. Snow, staring after her.

It rained the next time Pollyanna saw the Man. She greeted him, however, with a bright smile.

"It isn't so nice today, is it?" she called gleefully. "I'm glad it doesn't rain always!"

The Man stopped, with a scowl on his face.

"See here, little girl, we might just as well settle this once and for all. I've got something besides the weather to think of. I don't know whether the sun shines or not."

Pollyanna smiled. "No, sir, I thought you didn't. That's why I told you, so you would notice that the sun shines. I knew you'd be glad it did if you stopped to think of it!"

"Well, of all the—" he exclaimed, as he turned and strode on as before.

The next time Pollyanna met the Man, his eyes were gazing straight into hers.

"Good afternoon," he greeted her a little stiffly. "I *know* the sun is shining today."

The Man always spoke to Pollyanna after this, though usually he said just "Good afternoon." Even that, however, was a great surprise to Nancy, who was with Pollyanna one day when he passed.

"Sakes alive, Miss Pollyanna," she gasped, "did that man *speak to you*? Do you know who he is?"

Pollyanna frowned and shook her head.

"He hasn't spoken to anybody for years, child, except when he just has to. He's John Pendleton. He lives by himself in the big house on Pendleton Hill. He's got loads of money. Nobody in town is as rich as he is. But he ain't spending his money. He's a-savin' it."

"Oh, for the poor people," Pollyanna decided. "How perfectly splendid!"

Several days later, Pollyanna went to see Mrs. Snow and found her again in a darkened room.

"Oh, it's you, is it?" asked a fretful voice from the bed. "I wish you had come yesterday. I *wanted* you yesterday."

"Did you? Well, I'm glad 'tisn't any farther away from yesterday than today is, then," laughed Pollyanna. She came cheerily into the room and set her basket carefully down on a chair. "How do you do today?"

"Very poorly, thank you," murmured Mrs. Snow. "I haven't been able to nap all day."

Polly nodded sympathetically.

"I almost forgot—but I've thought it up, Mrs. Snow—what you can be glad about."

"*Glad* about! What do you mean?"

"Why, don't you remember? You asked me to tell you something to be glad about—even though you did have to lie here in bed all day."

"Oh!" scoffed the woman. "*That?* Yes, I remember that. But I didn't suppose you were serious about it."

"Oh, yes, I was," nodded Pollyanna, "and I found it, too."

"Did you, really? Well, what is it?"

Pollyanna drew a long breath.

"I thought how glad you could be that other folks weren't like you—all sick in bed like this, you know," she announced.

Mrs. Snow stared. Her eyes were angry.

"Well, really!" she exclaimed.

"And now I'll tell you the game," said Pollyanna cheerfully. And she began to tell of the missionary barrel, the crutches, and the doll that did not come.

The story was just finished when Milly appeared at the door.

"Your aunt is wanting you, Miss Pollyanna. She says you're to hurry—that you've got some practicing to make up before dark."

Pollyanna rose reluctantly.

"All right," she sighed. "I'll hurry." Suddenly she laughed. "I suppose I ought to be glad I've got legs to hurry with, hadn't I, Mrs. Snow? Good-bye!"

There was no answer. Mrs. Snow's eyes were closed. But Milly, whose eyes were wide open with surprise, saw that there were tears on the pale, thin cheeks.

# CHAPTER FIVE

## *Pollyanna to the Rescue*

August came. August brought several surprises and some changes—none of which really surprised Nancy. Ever since Pollyanna's arrival, Nancy had looked for surprises and changes.

First there was the kitten Pollyanna found mewing down the road and brought home.

"And I was glad I didn't find anyone who owned it," she told her aunt happily. "I love kitties. I knew you'd be glad to let it live here."

Miss Polly opened her lips and tried to speak—but she could think of nothing to say. She was held fast by the same helpless feeling that had been hers so often since Pollyanna's arrival.

The next day it was a dog, even dirtier and sadder, perhaps, than the kitten. Again Miss Polly found herself as the kind protector and angel of mercy. And she was a woman who disliked dogs even more than cats, if possible!

However, when, in less than a week, Pollyanna brought home a small, ragged boy, Miss Polly *did* have something to say.

On a pleasant Thursday morning, Pollyanna had been taking food again to Mrs. Snow. Mrs. Snow and Pollyanna were the best of friends now, and she and Mrs. Snow were playing the "glad game" together. Mrs. Snow had been sorry for everything for so long that it was not easy to be glad for anything now. But under Pollyanna's cheery instruction and merry laughter at her mistakes, she was learning fast.

Pollyanna was thinking of this now when suddenly she saw the boy, sitting in a hopeless little heap by the roadside, whittling half-heartedly at a small stick.

"Hullo," smiled Pollyanna.

The boy glanced up, but he looked away again, at once.

"Hullo yourself," he mumbled.

Pollyanna hesitated, then dropped herself comfortably down on the grass near him.

"My name's Pollyanna Whittier," she began pleasantly. "What's yours?"

The boy stirred restlessly. He even almost got to his feet. But he settled back.

"Jimmy Bean," he grunted.

"Good! Now we're introduced. I live at Miss Polly Harrington's house. Where do you live?"

"Nowhere."

"Nowhere! Why, everybody lives somewhere," said Pollyanna.

"Well, I don't—just now. I'm a-huntin' up a new place."

"Oh! Where is it?"

"Silly! I wouldn't be huntin' if I knew!"

Pollyanna tossed her head. This was not a nice boy, and she did not like to be called "silly." Still, he was somebody besides old folks. "Where did you live before?" she asked.

The boy gave a short laugh, but his face looked a little pleasanter when he spoke this time.

"I'm Jimmy Bean, and I'm ten years old goin' on eleven. I come last year to live at the Orphans' Home. They've got so many kids, though, there ain't much room for me. I'd *like* a home. If ye has a home, ye has folks, an' I ain't had folks since my dad died. I've tried four houses, but they didn't want me."

"Oh, dear! I know just how you feel," said Pollyanna. "After my father died there wasn't anybody for me till Aunt Polly said she'd take—" Pollyanna stopped. She had a wonderful idea.

"Oh, I know just the place for you," she cried. "Aunt Polly'll take you—I know she will! Didn't she take me? And didn't she take Fluffy and Buffy? And they're only cats and dogs. You don't know how good and kind she is!"

Pollyanna quickly led her companion straight into the presence of her amazed aunt.

"Oh, Aunt Polly," she beamed, "just look here! I've got something ever so much nicer than Fluffy and Buffy for you to bring up. It's a real live boy. He won't mind a bit sleeping in the attic and he says he'll work."

Miss Polly grew white, then very red.

"Pollyanna, who is this dirty little boy? Where did you find him?" she demanded sharply.

The "dirty little boy" fell back a step and looked toward the door. Pollyanna laughed merrily.

"There, I forgot to tell you his name! This is Jimmy Bean, Aunt Polly."

"Well, what is he doing here?"

"Why, Aunt Polly, I just told you! He's for you. I brought him home so he could live here. I told him how good you were to me, and to Fluffy and Buffy. I knew you would be to him, because of course he's even nicer than cats and dogs…"

"That will *do*, Pollyanna! This is the most absurd thing you've done yet. As if tramp cats and mangy dogs weren't bad enough, you must bring home ragged little beggars from the street!"

The boy's eyes flashed and his chin came up. "I ain't a beggar, ma'am!" he stormed. With two strides of his sturdy little legs he left the room.

"Oh, Aunt Polly," choked Pollyanna. "Why, I thought you'd be *glad* to have him here! Oh!" She broke off, hurrying blindly from the room.

Before the boy had reached the end of the driveway, Pollyanna caught up to him.

"Boy! Boy! Jimmy Bean, I want you to know how sorry I am," she panted.

"Sorry nothin'! I ain't blamin' you," replied the boy. "But I ain't no beggar."

"Of course you aren't! But you mustn't blame Auntie," appealed Pollyanna. "She is good and kind. I probably didn't explain it right. I do wish I could find some place for you, though!"

The little boy shrugged his shoulders and turned away.

Pollyanna did not turn her steps toward home. She was sure that nothing would do her quite as much good as a walk through the green quiet of Pendleton Woods. Suddenly Pollyanna lifted her head and listened. A dog had barked some distance ahead. A moment later he came dashing toward her, still barking.

"Hullo, doggie—hullo!" Pollyanna snapped her fingers at the dog and looked down the path. She had seen the dog once before, with the Man, Mr. John Pendleton. For some minutes she watched eagerly, but he did not appear. Then she turned her attention toward the dog.

He was acting strangely, giving short, sharp yelps of alarm, running back and forth in the path ahead. At last Pollyanna understood, turned, and followed him.

It was not long before Pollyanna came upon the reason for it all. A man was lying motionless at the foot of a steep, overhanging rock a few yards from the path. With a cry of dismay Pollyanna ran to his side.

"Mr. Pendleton! Oh, are you hurt?"

"Hurt? Oh, no! I'm just taking a nap in the sunshine," snapped the Man. "There, there, child, I beg your pardon. It's only this confounded leg of mine." He paused, and with some difficulty reached into a pocket and then handed her a key.

"Now, listen. Straight through the path, about five minutes' walk, is my house. On the big desk you'll find a telephone. Call Dr. Thomas Chilton and tell him that John Pendleton is at the foot of Little Eagle Ledge with a broken leg. He'll know what to do."

With a little sobbing cry, Pollyanna went. It was not long before she came in sight of the gray stone mansion. She sped across the untidy lawn and around to the side door. Her fingers were stiff from clutching the keys so tightly, but at last the heavy, carved door swung slowly open.

Pollyanna ran through the hall to the door at the end and opened it. The room was large, dark and somber. Through the west window the sun's rays shone gold across the floor and the tarnished brass of the fireplace. The walls were lined with books. The floor was littered with paper. Everywhere was dust, dust, dust. In the middle of the room was the large desk with the telephone.

In due time she had Dr. Chilton himself at the other end of the phone. She fearfully delivered her message and answered the doctor's short, direct questions. This done, she hung up the receiver and drew a long breath of relief.

In what seemed, even to the injured man, an incredibly short time, Pollyanna was back in the woods at the man's side.

"The doctor will be right up just as soon as possible with the men and things," she said. "He knew just where you were, so I came back here. I wanted to be with you to hold your head."

"You are so kind, even though I'm…" said the Man, wincing with pain.

"Even though you're so—cross?" said the girl.

"Thanks for your honesty. Yes."

Pollyanna laughed. "But you're only cross on the *outside*. You aren't cross on the inside one bit. I can tell by the way this dog loves you."

Minutes passed and the sky darkened. At last the dog perked up his ears and gave a short, sharp bark. Pollyanna heard voices, and very soon three men appeared with a stretcher. The tallest was a smooth-shaven, kind-eyed man whom Pollyanna knew by sight as "Dr. Chilton."

"Well, my little lady, playing nurse?" the doctor asked cheerily.

"Oh, no, sir," smiled Pollyanna. "I've only held his head. But I'm glad I was here."

"So am I," nodded Dr. Chilton, as he turned his attention to the injured man.

---

Pollyanna was a little late for supper on the night of the accident to John Pendleton, but as it happened she escaped without punishment.

Nancy met her at the door and explained that Aunt Polly had been called out of town for a few days to attend a funeral.

Then, with an open mouth and wide eyes, Nancy listened to Pollyanna tell of the accident—and about her being inside that big, dreary, gray stone house!

# CHAPTER SIX

## *Just a Matter of Jelly*

It was about a week after the accident in Pendleton Woods that Pollyanna said to her aunt one morning, "Aunt Polly, please would you mind if I took Mrs. Snow's calf's-foot jelly this week to someone else? You let me take jelly to *her*, so I thought you would to *him*—this once. His broken leg won't last forever, and she can have all the rest of the things after just once or twice."

"He? Broken leg? What are you talking about, Pollyanna?"

Pollyanna stared. Then her face relaxed.

"Oh, I forgot you didn't know. I found him in the woods, and I had to unlock his house and

telephone for the men and the doctor, and hold his head, and everything. And then I came away and haven't seen him since. So I thought how nice it would be if I could take the calf's-foot jelly to him just this once. Aunt Polly, may I?"

"Yes, yes, I suppose so," agreed Miss Polly. "Who did you say he was?"

"The Man. I mean, Mr. John Pendleton."

Miss Polly almost sprang from her chair.

"*John Pendleton!*"

"Yes. Nancy told me his name. Maybe you know him."

Miss Polly did not answer. Instead she asked, "Do *you* know him?"

"Oh, yes. He always speaks and smiles—now. I'll go and get the jelly," finished Pollyanna, already halfway across the room.

"Pollyanna, wait!" Miss Polly's voice was suddenly very stern. "I've changed my mind. I would prefer that Mrs. Snow had that jelly today. I do not care to send it to John Pendleton."

Pollyanna's face fell. "I know, he is cross—outside," she admitted sadly, "and I suppose you don't like him. But I wouldn't say 'twas you who sent it. I'd say 'twas me."

Miss Polly began to shake her head again. Then, suddenly, she stopped, and asked quietly, "Does he know who you are, Pollyanna? Does he know you are my niece?"

The little girl sighed. "I reckon not."

Miss Polly was looking at Pollyanna with eyes that did not seem to see her at all. Then she pulled herself up stiffly.

"Very well, Pollyanna," she said at last. "You may take the jelly to Mr. Pendleton as your gift. But be very sure that he does not think I sent it!"

"Thank you, Aunt Polly," exulted Pollyanna, as she flew through the door.

John Pendleton's great house looked very different to Pollyanna when she made her second visit. Windows were open. An elderly woman was hanging out clothes in the back yard. The doctor's carriage stood near the door.

A familiar small dog bounded up the steps to greet her. After a slight delay the woman who had been hanging out the clothes opened the door.

"If you please, I've brought some calf's-foot jelly for Mr. Pendleton," smiled Pollyanna.

The doctor, coming into the hall, stepped quickly forward.

"Ah! Some calf's-foot jelly?" he asked. "Fine! Maybe you'd like to see our patient, eh?"

"Oh, yes, sir," beamed Pollyanna, and a few moments later found herself alone with a very cross-looking man lying flat on his back in bed.

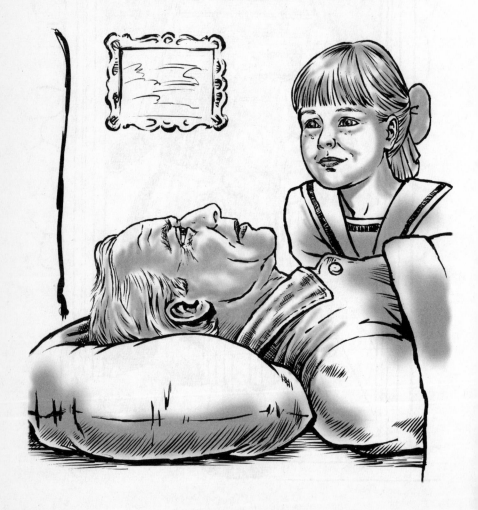

"See here, didn't I say—" began an angry voice. "Oh, it's you!" it broke off, as Pollyanna walked toward the bed. In spite of himself the man smiled, but all he said was "Humph!"

"I've brought you some jelly," said Pollyanna. "I hope you like it."

"Yes, yes, well. I'm flat on my back right here this minute, and I'll probably stay here till doomsday, I guess."

Pollyanna looked shocked.

"Oh, no! Broken legs don't last, and you didn't break but one. You can be glad 'twasn't two."

"Of course! So fortunate," sniffed the man, with uplifted eyebrows. "I suppose I might be glad I wasn't a centipede and didn't break fifty!"

Pollyanna chuckled and sat on the bed.

"Oh, of course," the man went on, "I can be glad, too, for all the rest, I suppose—the nurse, and the doctor, and that woman in the kitchen!"

"Why, yes, sir! Think how bad 'twould be if you *didn't* have them—you lying here like this!"

"You expect me to be glad for a woman who rearranges my house? And a man who aids her, and calls it 'nursing'? And a doctor who eggs 'em on? And they all expect me to pay them for it!"

Pollyanna frowned sympathetically.

"Yes, I know. *That* part is too bad—about the money—when you've been saving it all this time."

"Child, what are you talking about?"

Pollyanna smiled radiantly.

"About your money, you know, and saving it for the poor. You see, I found out about it. Nancy told me."

The man's jaw dropped.

"Well, may I inquire who Nancy is?"

"Our Nancy. She works for Aunt Polly, Polly Harrington. I live with her."

The man made a sudden movement.

"Miss—Polly—Harrington!" he breathed. "You live with *her?*"

"Yes. She's taken me to bring up on account of my mother, you know," faltered Pollyanna. "She's my mother's sister. After Father went to be with Mother in Heaven, there wasn't anyone left for me. So Aunt Polly took me."

The man did not answer. His face was so white that Pollyanna was frightened. She rose timidly to her feet

"I reckon maybe I'd better go now," she said quietly. "I hope you'll like the jelly."

The man turned his head suddenly, and opened his eyes. He said gently, "And so you are Miss Polly Harrington's niece?"

"Yes, sir."

John Pendleton's lips curved in an odd smile. He said slowly, "But you can't mean that it was Miss Polly Harrington who sent that jelly to me?"

Pollyanna looked distressed.

"N-no, sir, she didn't. She said I must be very sure not to let you think she did send it."

"I thought as much," stated the man, turning away his head. And Pollyanna, still more distressed, tiptoed from the room.

Pollyanna was not the only one distressed that day. Aunt Polly seemed quite distressed when Pollyanna told her that Dr. Chilton had given her a ride home from Mr. Pendleton's. And she was even *more* distressed when Pollyanna announced:

"Don't worry, Aunt Polly. I told Mr. Pendleton that *you* most certainly did not send the jelly!"

# CHAPTER SEVEN

## A Red Rose and a Lace Shawl

One rainy day, Miss Polly went to a meeting of the Ladies' Aid Society. When she returned, her cheeks were a bright, pretty pink, and her hair, blown by the damp wind, had fluffed into curls. Pollyanna had never seen her aunt look like this.

"Oh—oh! Why, Aunt Polly, you've got 'em, too," she cried joyfully, dancing around her aunt.

"Got what, you impossible child?"

"No, no, please, Aunt Polly! Don't smooth 'em out! Those darling little black curls. Oh, please, may I do your hair like I did Mrs. Snow's, and put in a flower? Why, you'd be ever so much prettier! You *will* let me do your hair, won't you?"

"Pollyanna!" Miss Polly spoke very sharply. Yet, Pollyanna's words had given her an odd feeling of joy. When before had anybody cared how she, or her hair, looked? When before had anybody "loved" to see her "pretty"?

"You didn't say I *couldn't* do your hair," Pollyanna crowed. "Now wait just where you are. I'll get a comb."

"But, Pollyanna, I—I—" But to her amazement, Miss Polly found herself in a chair with Pollyanna eagerly primping and fussing over her.

"Oh, my! what pretty hair you've got," chattered Pollyanna, "and there's so much more of it than Mrs. Snow has, too! Why, Aunt Polly, I'll make you so pretty everybody'll just love to look at you!"

"Pollyanna!" gasped a voice from a veil of hair. "I—I'm sure I don't know why I'm letting you do this silly thing."

"But, Aunt Polly—don't you like to look at pretty things? Now don't peek—I'll be right back!"

But, of course, Miss Polly *did* peek. She caught a glimpse of herself in the mirror of the dressing table. What she saw sent a flush of rosy color to her cheeks.

She saw a face—not young, it is true—but alight with excitement and surprise. The cheeks were a pretty pink. The eyes sparkled. The dark hair lay in loose waves about the forehead. It curved back over the ears, with softening little curls here and there.

Pollyanna rushed back in with a beautiful shawl, yellowed from being packed away, and scented with lavender. With trembling fingers, Pollyanna draped it about her aunt's shoulders. One touch was still needed. She pulled her aunt toward the sun parlor where she could see a red rose blooming within reach of her hand.

"Only a minute! I'll have you ready now quicker'n no time," panted Pollyanna, reaching for the rose and thrusting it into the soft hair above Miss Polly's ear. "There!"

For one dazed moment Miss Polly looked at herself. Then, something out the open windows of the sun parlor made her give a low cry and flee to her room. It was Dr. Chilton's horse and carriage turning into the driveway.

Delightedly, Pollyanna called out, "Dr. Chilton! Did you want to see me? I'm up here."

"Yes!" he said. "Will you come down, please?"

In the bedroom Pollyanna found a flushed-faced, angry-eyed woman plucking at the pins that held a lace shawl in place.

"Pollyanna, how could you?" moaned the woman. "Letting me be seen like this!"

"But you looked lovely, perfectly lovely, Aunt Polly, and—"

The woman flung the shawl to one side and attacked her hair with shaking fingers.

"Oh, dear! And you did look so pretty," sobbed Pollyanna, as she stumbled through the door and sped downstairs to the waiting doctor.

"I've prescribed you for a patient," announced the doctor, "and he's sent me to get the prescription filled. Mr. John Pendleton would like to see you today. Will you come? I'll call for you and bring you back before six o'clock."

"I'd love to! Let me ask Aunt Polly," cried the girl. In a few moments she returned, hat in hand.

"Wasn't it your aunt I saw with you a few minutes ago in the window of the sun parlor?" the doctor asked as they drove away.

Pollyanna drew a long breath.

"Yes, but she's troubled. I dressed her up in a perfectly lovely lace shawl I found upstairs, and

I fixed her hair and put in a rose. She looked so pretty. Didn't *you* think she looked just lovely?"

For a moment the doctor did not answer. When he did speak his voice was so low Pollyanna could barely hear the words.

"Yes, Pollyanna, I thought she did look lovely."

"Did you? I'm so glad! I'll tell her," nodded the little girl.

To her surprise the doctor said, "Pollyanna, I'm afraid I have to ask you not to tell her that."

"Why, Dr. Chilton! Why not? I should think you'd be glad—"

"But she might not be," cut in the doctor.

Pollyanna considered this for a moment.

"Well, maybe she wouldn't," she sighed. "I remember now. It was because she saw you that she ran."

The doctor said nothing. He did not speak again, indeed, until they were almost to the great stone house in which John Pendleton lay with a broken leg.

# CHAPTER EIGHT

## *"A Mystery"*

Mr. Pendleton greeted Pollyanna with a smile.
"Well, Miss Pollyanna, I'm thinking you must
be a very forgiving little person, or you wouldn't
have come to see me today."

"Why, Mr. Pendleton, I was real glad to come,
and I'm sure I don't see why I shouldn't be."

"Oh, well, I was pretty cross with you, I'm
afraid, the other day when you so kindly brought
me the jelly—and that time you found me with the
broken leg. I don't think I've ever thanked you."

"But I was glad to find you. That is, I don't
mean I was glad your leg was broken, of course,"
she corrected hurriedly.

John Pendleton smiled.

"I understand and I consider you a very brave little girl to do what you did that day. I thank you for the jelly, too," he added in a lighter voice.

"Did you like it?" asked Pollyanna.

"Very much. I suppose there isn't any more today that Aunt Polly *didn't* send, is there?" he asked with an awkward smile.

"N-no, sir," stammered Pollyanna, blushing. "Please, sir, I didn't mean to be rude the other day when I said Aunt Polly did *not* send the jelly."

"Well, well, this will never do at all! I sent for you so we could have some fun. Listen! Out in the library you will find a carved box in the big case near the fireplace. You may bring it to me. It is heavy, but not too heavy for you to carry."

"Oh, I'm awfully strong," declared Pollyanna cheerfully, as she sprang to her feet. In a minute she had returned with the box.

It was a wonderful half-hour that Pollyanna spent then. The box was full of treasures that John Pendleton had picked up in years of travel. Each had some entertaining story, whether it was carved chessmen from China, or a little jade idol from India.

The visit was delightful. Before it was over, they were talking about Pollyanna's daily life, Nancy, and even Aunt Polly. They were talking, too, of life and home long ago in the faraway Western town.

When it was nearly time for her to go, the man said, in a voice Pollyanna had never before heard from stern John Pendleton:

"I want you to come to see me often. Will you? I'm lonesome, and I need you. There's another reason, too. I thought, after I found out who you were, that I didn't want you to come anymore. You reminded me of something I have tried to forget... But after a time I was wanting to see you so much. Not seeing you was making me remember the thing I wanted to forget. So now I want you to come visit. Will you—little girl?"

Pollyanna's eyes beamed with sympathy for the sad-faced man before her.

"Why, yes, Mr. Pendleton," she said. "I'd love to come visit you!"

After supper that evening, Pollyanna sat with Nancy on the back porch. She told her all about Mr. John Pendleton's wonderful carved box, and the still more wonderful things it contained.

"I don't see why everybody thinks he's so bad, Nancy," Pollyanna said. "They wouldn't, if they knew him. But even Aunt Polly doesn't like him very well."

"What beats me is how he took to you so, Miss Pollyanna," Nancy said. "He ain't the sort o' man what gen'rally takes to kids, he ain't, he ain't."

Pollyanna smiled.

"I reckon he didn't want to *all* the time. Why, only today he said that once he felt he never wanted to see me again, because I reminded him of something he wanted to forget."

"What's that?" interrupted Nancy excitedly. "He said ye reminded him of something he wanted to forget?"

"He didn't tell me what. He just said it was something."

"*A mystery!*" breathed Nancy, in an awestruck voice. "Oh, Miss Pollyanna!"

The next minute she was down at Pollyanna's side. "Tell me. It was after he found out ye was Miss Polly's niece that he didn't ever want to see ye again, wasn't it? And Miss Polly wouldn't send the jelly herself, would she?"

"No."

"And he began to act strangely after he found out ye was her niece, didn't he?"

"Why, y-yes, he did act a little odd," admitted Pollyanna, with a thoughtful frown.

Nancy drew a long sigh.

"Then I've got it, sure! *Mr. John Pendleton was Miss Polly Harrington's beloved!*" she announced.

"Why, Nancy, he couldn't be! She doesn't like him," objected Pollyanna.

"Of course she don't! *That's* the quarrel!"

Pollyanna looked doubtful. Nancy happily settled herself to tell the story.

"It's like this. Just before you come, Mr. Tom told me Miss Polly was in love once. I didn't believe it. But Mr. Tom said she was, and that her beloved was livin' now right in this town. And *now* I know, of course. It's John Pendleton."

Pollyanna *still* looked doubtful.

"Ain't he got a mystery in his life? Don't he shut himself up in that grand house alone, and never speak to no one? Didn't he act odd when he found out ye was Miss Polly's niece? And now ain't he owned up that ye remind him of somethin' he wants to forget? Why, Miss Pollyanna, it's as plain as the nose on yer face!"

"Oh-h!" breathed Pollyanna, in wide-eyed amazement. "But, Nancy, I should think if they loved each other they'd make up sometime. Both of 'em all alone all these years. I should think they'd be glad to make up!"

Nancy chuckled.

"Miss Pollyanna, it would be a pretty slick piece of business if you could *get* them to make up. Wouldn't folks stare some—Miss Polly and him! I guess, though, there ain't much chance!"

Pollyanna said nothing, but when she went into the house a little later, her face was very thoughtful.

# CHAPTER NINE

## *Prisms*

As the warm August days passed, Pollyanna went often to the great house on Pendleton Hill. But though the man sent for her frequently, when she was there he did not seem much happier.

She had twice tried to tell him about the "glad game." But neither time had she gotten beyond the beginning of what her father had said before John Pendleton turned the conversation to another subject.

Pollyanna never doubted now that John Pendleton was her Aunt Polly's one-time beloved. With all the strength of her heart, she wished she could bring happiness into their lonely lives.

Just how she was to do this, however, she could not see. She talked to Mr. Pendleton about her aunt. He listened, sometimes politely, sometimes irritably, often with a quizzical smile.

She tried to talk to her aunt about Mr. Pendleton, but Miss Polly would not listen. She always found something else to talk about. She also did that when Pollyanna was talking of others—Pollyanna's father, or Dr. Chilton, for instance. Aunt Polly seemed bitter against Dr. Chilton, as Pollyanna found out one day when a bad cold kept her shut up in the house.

"If you are not better by night I shall send for the doctor," Aunt Polly said.

"Then I'm going to be worse," Pollyanna laughed. "I'd love for Dr. Chilton to come see me!"

Aunt Polly blushed. "It will not be Dr. Chilton, Pollyanna," she said sternly. "Dr. Chilton is not our family physician. I shall send for Dr. Warren."

Pollyanna did not grow worse, however, and Dr. Warren was not summoned.

Early one morning, toward the end of August, Pollyanna called on Mr. Pendleton. It was then she found the flaming band of blue and gold and green edged with red and violet lying across his pillow.

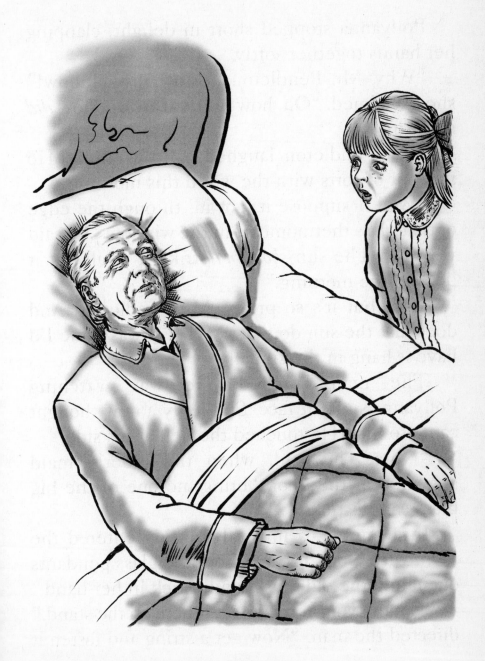

Pollyanna stopped short in delight, clapping her hands together softly.

"Why, Mr. Pendleton, it's a baby rainbow!" she exclaimed. "Oh, how pretty it is! But how *did* it get in?"

John Pendleton laughed a little grimly. He was out of sorts with the world this morning.

"Well, I suppose it 'got in' through the edge of that glass thermometer in the window," he said wearily. "The sun *shouldn't* strike it at all but it does in the morning."

"Oh, but it's so pretty, Mr. Pendleton! And does just the sun do that? My! If it was mine I'd have it hang in the sun all day long!"

The man laughed. He was watching Pollyanna's intent face. Suddenly a new thought came to him. He touched the bell at his side.

"Nora," he said, when the elderly maid appeared at the door, "bring me one of the big brass candlesticks."

In a minute, a musical tinkling entered the room with Nora. It came from the glass pendants encircling the old brass candlestick in her hand.

"Thank you. You may set it here on the stand," directed the man. "Now get a string and fasten it to that window there. Let the string reach straight across the window from side to side. That will be all. Thank you," he said, when she had carried out his directions.

"Bring me the candlestick now, please, Pollyanna."

In a moment he was slipping off the pendants, one by one, until a dozen of them lay on the bed.

"Now, my dear, hook them to that little string Nora fastened across the window."

Pollyanna hung up three of the pendants in the sunlit window—and then saw what was going to happen. She was so excited she could scarcely control her shaking fingers enough to hang up the rest. But at last she was finished, and she stepped back with a low cry of delight.

The dreary bedroom had become a fairyland. Everywhere were bits of dancing red and green, violet and orange, gold and blue. The wall, the floor, and the furniture, even the bed itself, were aflame with shimmering bits of color.

"Oh, how lovely!" breathed Pollyanna. "How I would like to give them to Aunt Polly and Mrs. Snow and—lots of folks. I reckon *then* they'd be glad all right!"

Mr. Pendleton laughed.

"Oh, I forgot," Pollyanna said suddenly, "you don't know about the game."

"Suppose you tell me, then."

And this time Pollyanna told him. She told him the whole thing from the very first—from the crutches that should have been a doll. As she talked, she did not look at his face. Her eyes were still on the dancing flecks of color from the prism pendants swaying in the sunlit window.

"And that's all," she sighed. "And I think the sun is trying to play it—the game."

For a moment there was silence. Then Mr. Pendleton said in a low voice, "Perhaps. But I'm thinking that the very finest prism of them all is yourself, Pollyanna."

# CHAPTER TEN

## *Surprises*

Pollyanna entered school in September. She was well advanced for a girl of her years, and she was soon a happy member of a class of girls and boys her own age.

School, in some ways, was a surprise to Pollyanna. Pollyanna, certainly, was very much of a surprise to school. They were soon on the best of terms, however. Pollyanna confessed to her aunt that going to school *was* living, after all—though she had had her doubts before.

In spite of her delight in her new work, Pollyanna did not forget her old friends. She visited them as often as she could.

But John Pendleton did not seem satisfied. One Saturday afternoon, while they were sitting in the great library, he spoke to her about it.

"Pollyanna, how would you like to come and live with me?" he asked. "I don't see anything of you, nowadays."

Pollyanna laughed. Mr. Pendleton was such a funny man! "I thought you didn't like to have folks 'round," she said.

He smiled.

"Oh, but that was before you taught me to play that wonderful game of yours. Now I'm glad to be waited on, hand and foot!" He picked up one of the crutches at his side and playfully shook it at the little girl.

"Oh, but you aren't *really* glad at all for things. You just *say* you are," pouted Pollyanna. "You know you don't play the game right *ever*, Mr. Pendleton—you know you don't!"

The man's face grew suddenly very grave.

"That's why I want you around, little girl—to help me play it. Will you come live here?"

Pollyanna turned in surprise.

"Why, Mr. Pendleton, I can't. You know I can't. Why, I'm Aunt Polly's!"

Something crossed the man's face that Pollyanna could not quite understand. His head came up almost fiercely. But then he said gently, "Perhaps she *would* let you live here. Would you come, if she did?"

Now his voice was low and very sad.

"Pollyanna, long years ago I loved somebody very much. I hoped to bring her to this house. I pictured how happy we'd be together in our home all the long years to come."

"Yes," pitied Pollyanna, her eyes shining with sympathy.

"But I didn't bring her here. Never mind why. And ever since then this great gray pile of stone has been a house—never a home. It takes a woman's hand and heart, or a child's presence, to make a home, Pollyanna. I have not had either. Now will you come, my dear?"

Pollyanna sprang to her feet. Her face was fairly shining.

"Oh, Mr. Pendleton, you mean that you wish you had had that woman's hand and heart all this time?"

"Why, y-yes, Pollyanna."

"I'm so glad! Then it's all right," she sighed.

"Now you can take us both, and everything will be lovely. Aunt Polly isn't won over, yet. But I'm sure she will be if you tell it to her just as you did to me, and then we'd both come, of course."

A look of terror leaped to the man's eyes.

"Aunt Polly come—*here*?"

Pollyanna's eyes widened a little.

"Would you rather go *there*? Of course the house isn't quite so pretty, but it's nearer—"

"Pollyanna, what *are* you talking about?" asked the man, very gently now.

"Why, about where we're going to live, of course," said Pollyanna, in surprise. "I *thought* you meant here, at first. You said it was here that you had wanted Aunt Polly's hand and heart all these years to make a home, and—"

The man raised his hand and began to speak, but the next moment he dropped it at his side.

Nora came in to announce: "The doctor, sir."

John Pendleton turned to Pollyanna quickly.

"Pollyanna, for Heaven's sake, say nothing of what I asked you—yet," he begged, in a low voice.

Pollyanna dimpled into a sunny smile. "Of course not! I know you'd rather tell her yourself!" she called back merrily over her shoulder.

# CHAPTER ELEVEN

## *And More Surprises*

The next Sunday morning, Dr. Chilton caught up to Pollyanna in his carriage as she was walking home from church.

"Let me drive you home, Pollyanna. I want to speak to you a minute. I was just driving over to your place. Mr. Pendleton sent a special request for you to see him this afternoon. He says it's very important."

Pollyanna nodded happily. "Yes, it is! I'll go."

The doctor's eyes twinkled. "I'm not sure I should let you go, young lady. Mr. Pendleton seemed upset from your last visit—and you're supposed to be his medicine."

Pollyanna laughed. "Oh, it wasn't me! It was my Aunt Polly!"

"Your—aunt?"

Pollyanna gave a happy bounce in her seat.

"Yes. And it's so exciting and lovely, just like a story, you know. I—I'm going to tell you. You see, he's in love with her—"

"Love!?" the doctor exclaimed.

"Yes," nodded Pollyanna happily. "That's the story part, you see. I didn't know it till Nancy told me. She said Aunt Polly had a beloved years ago—until they quarreled. Nancy did not know who it was, but now we do! It's Mr. Pendleton, you know."

The reins fell limp in the doctor's hands as the carriage pulled up to the Harrington house.

"Oh. No, I didn't know," he said quietly.

Pollyanna went over that afternoon to John Pendleton's house. He looked very nervous when the young girl arrived. He said at once, "Pollyanna, I've been trying all night to puzzle out what you meant about my wanting your Aunt Polly's hand and heart. What did you mean?"

"Why, because you were in love once. And I'm so glad you still feel that way now."

"In love!—Your Aunt Polly and I?"
Pollyanna opened her eyes wide.

"Why, Nancy said you were!"

The man gave a short laugh. "Well, I'm afraid
Nancy didn't know."

"Then you weren't in love?" Pollyanna's
voice was tragic with dismay.

"Never!"

"And it *isn't* all coming out like a book? Oh,
dear! And it was all going so splendidly," sobbed
Pollyanna. "I'd have been so glad to come—with
Aunt Polly."

"And you won't—now?" The man asked the
question without turning his head.

"Of course not! I'm Aunt Polly's."

The man turned now, almost fiercely.

"Before you were hers, Pollyanna, you were
your mother's. And it was your mother's hand and
heart that I wanted long years ago."

"My mother's?"

"Yes. I had not meant to tell you, but perhaps
it's better that I do now."

John Pendleton's face had grown very white.

"I loved your mother, but she didn't love me.

She married your father. I did not know until then how much I did care. Since then I have been a cross, crabbed, unlovable, unloved old man—though I'm not even sixty yet. Then, one day you danced into my life and brightened my dreary old world with your cheeriness. I thought I never wanted to see you again, because I didn't want to be reminded of your mother. But now I want you always. Pollyanna, won't you come *now*?"

"But, Mr. Pendleton, there's Aunt Polly!" Pollyanna's eyes were blurred with tears.

"What about me? How do you suppose I'm going to be 'glad' about anything—without you? It's only since you came that I've been glad to live! But if I had you for my own little girl, I'd be glad for—anything. And all my money, to the last cent, would go to make you happy."

"Anybody with as much money as you have doesn't need *me* to make you glad about things," smiled Pollyanna. "You're making other folks so glad giving them things that you just can't help being glad yourself! Why, look at those prisms you gave Mrs. Snow and me, and the gold piece you gave Nancy on her birthday, and—"

"What gladness there was, was because of you. *You* gave those things, not I!" he said. "And that only goes to prove all the more how I need you, little girl." His voice softened. "If ever, ever I am to play the 'glad game,' Pollyanna, you'll have to come and play it with me."

The little girl's forehead puckered into a frown.

"All right. I'll ask Aunt Polly," she said wistfully. "I don't mean that I wouldn't like to live here with you, Mr. Pendleton, but... Well, anyhow, I'm glad I didn't tell her yesterday."

The sky was darkening fast into a thunder shower when Pollyanna hurried down the hill from John Pendleton's house. Halfway home she met Nancy with an umbrella.

"Miss Polly wanted me to come with this. She was *worried* about ye!"

"Was she?" murmured Pollyanna.

"You don't seem to notice what I said," Nancy said. "I said yer aunt was *worried* about ye! *You* don't seem to sense what it means to have Miss Polly *worried* about ye, child! It means she's at last gettin' somewheres near human. An' that she ain't jest doin' her duty by ye all the time."

"Why, Nancy," objected Pollyanna, "Aunt Polly always does her duty. She a very dutiful woman!"

Nancy chuckled, "You're right she is—and she always was, I guess! But she's somethin' more, now, since you came."

"There, that's what I was going to ask you, Nancy," Pollyanna sighed, with a frown. "Do you think Aunt Polly likes to have me here? Would she mind—if—if I wasn't here any more?"

"As if that wasn't jest what I was tellin' ye!" Nancy cried. "Didn't she send me quickly with an umbrella 'cause she seen a little cloud in the sky? Didn't she make me tote yer things downstairs, so you could have the pretty room you wanted? It's little ways that show how you've been softenin' her up—the cat, and the dog, and the way she speaks to *me*. There ain't no tellin' how she'd miss ye if ye wasn't here," finished Nancy.

"Oh, Nancy. You don't know how glad I am that Aunt Polly wants me!"

"As if I'd leave her now!" thought Pollyanna, as she climbed the stairs to her room a little later. "I always knew I wanted to live with Aunt Polly. But maybe I didn't know quite how much I wanted Aunt Polly to want to live with *me*!"

The task of telling John Pendleton her decision would not be an easy one, Pollyanna knew, and she dreaded it. As soon as she could, she hurried to his house, and found herself in the great dim library. John Pendleton sat near her, his long, thin hands on the arms of his chair, and his faithful little dog at his feet.

"Well, Pollyanna, is it to be the 'glad game' with me, all the rest of my life?" asked the man gently.

"Oh, yes," cried Pollyanna. "I've thought of the very gladdest kind of a thing for you to do, and—"

"Pollyanna, you aren't going to say no!" interrupted a voice deep with emotion.

Pollyanna turned away her eyes. She could not meet the hurt, grieved gaze of her friend.

"So you didn't even ask your aunt!"

"You see, I found out without asking. Aunt Polly *wants* me with her, and—and I want to stay, too," she confessed bravely. "You don't know how good she's been to me. Oh, Mr. Pendleton, I *couldn't* leave Aunt Polly now!"

There was a long pause. Only the snapping of the wood fire in the grate broke the silence. At last, however, the man spoke.

"No. I see. You couldn't leave her now."

"Oh, but there is the very gladdest thing you *can* do, truly there is!" Pollyanna reminded him. "You said only a woman's hand and heart or a child's presence could make a home. And I can get you a child's presence—not me, you know, but another one."

"As if I would have any but you!"

"But you will, when you know. You're so kind and good! And, you'll like Jimmy Bean. I know you'll take him!"

"Take—*who*?"

"Jimmy Bean. He's the 'child's presence,' you know, and he'll be so glad to be it!"

"Will he? Well, I won't," exclaimed the man. "Pollyanna, this is sheer nonsense!"

"You don't mean you won't take him? He'd be a lovely child's presence," faltered Pollyanna. She was almost crying now. "And you *couldn't* be lonesome—with Jimmy around."

"Pollyanna, I suspect you are more right than you know," he said gently. "In fact, I *know* that a 'nice live little boy' would be far better than being lonesome. Suppose you tell me a little more about this nice little boy."

Perhaps Jimmy Bean's sad, sweet story as told by Pollyanna's eager little lips touched a heart already strangely softened. For when Pollyanna went home that night, she carried with her an invitation for Jimmy Bean himself to call at Mr. Pendleton's great, stone house with Pollyanna the next Saturday afternoon.

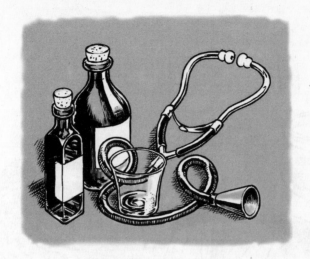

# CHAPTER TWELVE

## *The Accident*

At Mrs. Snow's request, Pollyanna went one day to Dr. Chilton's office to get the name of a medicine which Mrs. Snow had forgotten. As it chanced, Pollyanna had never before seen the inside of Dr. Chilton's office.

"I've never been to your home before! This *is* your home, isn't it?" she said, looking about her.

The doctor smiled a little sadly.

"Yes," he answered, "but it's a pretty poor apology for a home, Pollyanna. They're just rooms, that's all—not a home."

Pollyanna nodded her head wisely. Her eyes glowed with understanding.

"I know. It takes a woman's hand and heart, or a child's presence to make a home," she said. "Mr. Pendleton told me. Why don't you get a woman's hand and heart, Dr. Chilton? Or maybe you'd take Jimmy Bean—if Mr. Pendleton doesn't want him."

Dr. Chilton laughed.

"So Mr. Pendleton says it takes a woman's hand and heart to make a home, does he?" he asked curiously.

"Yes. Why don't you get a woman's hand and heart, Dr. Chilton?"

There was a moment's silence. Then very gravely the doctor said, "They're not always to be had for the asking, little girl."

Pollyanna frowned thoughtfully. Then her eyes widened in surprise.

"Why, Dr. Chilton, did you try to get somebody's hand and heart once, like Mr. Pendleton—and couldn't? Did you?"

The doctor got to his feet quickly and said, "Pollyanna, never mind about that now. Suppose you run back to Mrs. Snow. I've written down the name of the medicine. Was there anything else?"

Pollyanna shook her head as she turned toward the door.

It was on the last day of October that the accident occurred. Pollyanna, hurrying home from school, crossed the road at, she thought, a safe distance in front of a swiftly approaching car.

No one could tell afterward exactly what had happened, why it had happened, or who was to blame. But at five o'clock Pollyanna was carried, limp and unconscious, into her little room. There a white-faced Aunt Polly and a weeping Nancy undressed her tenderly and put her to bed. From the village, Dr. Warren was hurrying as fast as his car could bring him.

There appeared to be no bones broken, but the doctor looked very grave. He shook his head slowly and said that time alone could tell. A trained nurse was sent for. Aunt Polly's face grew even whiter. Nancy turned with a sob, and went back to her kitchen.

It was sometime the next morning that Pollyanna opened her eyes and realized where she was.

"Why, Aunt Polly, what's the matter? Isn't it daytime? Why don't I get up? Why, Aunt Polly, I can't get up," she moaned, falling back on the pillow. "What is the matter? Why can't I get up?"

Miss Polly's eyes looked up to the white-capped young woman standing in the window, out of the range of Pollyanna's eyes.

The young woman nodded.

"Tell her," the lips said.

Miss Polly cleared her throat, and tried to swallow the lump in her throat that would scarcely let her speak.

"You were hurt, dear, by an automobile last night. But never mind that now. Auntie wants you to rest and go to sleep again."

"Hurt? Oh, yes. I ran." Pollyanna's eyes were dazed. She lifted her hand to her forehead. "Why, it's bandaged and it hurts! Aunt Polly, I feel so funny, and so bad! My legs feel so strange—only they don't *feel* at all!"

Miss Polly struggled to her feet, and turned away. The nurse came forward quickly.

"Suppose you let me talk to you now," she began cheerily. "I am Miss Hunt, and I've come to help your aunt take care of you. And the very first thing I'm going to do is to ask you to swallow these little white pills for me."

Pollyanna's eyes grew a bit wild.

"But I don't want to be taken care of! I want to get up. Can't I go to school tomorrow?"

From the window where Aunt Polly now stood there came a half-stifled cry.

"Tomorrow?" smiled the nurse brightly. "Well, I may not let you out quite so soon as that, Miss Pollyanna. But just swallow these little pills for me, please, and we'll see what *they'll* do."

A minute later, Pollyanna spoke again. She spoke of school, and of the automobile, and of how her head ached. But very soon her voice trailed into silence as she drifted back into sleep.

# CHAPTER THIRTEEN

# *A Woman's Hand and Heart*

Pollyanna did not go to school next day or the day after that. But she did not realize this—or anything—very clearly until a week had passed. At last the fever went down, the pain lessened, and her mind awoke. She was then told again what had happened.

"So I am hurt, and not sick," she sighed at last. "Well, I'm glad of that."

"G-glad, Pollyanna?" asked her aunt who was sitting by her bed, holding her hand.

"Yes. I'd much rather have broken legs like Mr. Pendleton's than crippled ones like Mrs. Snow's. Broken legs get well, and crippled ones don't."

Miss Polly got suddenly to her feet and walked to the little dressing table across the room. Her face was white and drawn.

On the bed Pollyanna lay blinking at the dancing band of colors on the ceiling. It came from one of the prisms in the window.

"I'm glad it isn't smallpox, too," Pollyanna went on. "That would be worse than freckles. And I'm glad it isn't whooping cough or appendicitis or measles."

"You seem to be glad for a good many things, my dear," faltered Aunt Polly, putting her hand to her throat.

"I am." Pollyanna laughed softly. "I've been thinking of 'em—lots of 'em—all the time I've been looking up at that rainbow. I'm so glad Mr. Pendleton gave me those prisms. I'm glad of some things I haven't said yet. I don't know but I'm almost glad I was hurt."

"Pollyanna!"

Pollyanna laughed again. She turned bright eyes on her aunt. "Well, you see, since I have been hurt, you've called me 'dear' lots of times—and you didn't before. I love to be called 'dear.' Oh, Aunt Polly, I'm so glad you belong to me!"

Aunt Polly did not answer. Her hand was at her throat again. Her eyes were full of tears.

It was that afternoon that Nancy ran out to Old Tom, who was cleaning harnesses in the barn. Her eyes were wild.

"Mr. Tom, guess what's happened," she panted. "Who do you s'pose is in the parlor now with the mistress? It's—John Pendleton!"

Mr. John Pendleton did not have to wait long before a swift step warned him that Miss Polly was approaching. As he attempted to rise, she made a gesture of protest. She did not offer her hand, however, and her face was cold.

"I called to ask for—Pollyanna," he announced.

"Thank you. She is about the same," said Miss Polly. "Dr. Warren isn't quite sure what is wrong. He is in touch now with a New York specialist."

"But—but what *were* her injuries?"

"A slight cut on the head, one or two bruises, and an injury to the spine, which has seemed to cause paralysis from the hips down."

A low cry came from the man. There was a brief silence, then he asked, "And Pollyanna—how does she take it?"

"She doesn't know how things really are. She knows she can't move, but she thinks her legs are broken. She says she's glad it's broken legs like yours because broken legs get well. She talks like that all the time, until it seems as if I should die!"

It was this thought that made him ask very gently, as soon as he could control his voice, "I wonder if you know, Miss Harrington, how hard I tried to get Pollyanna to come and live with me. I wanted to adopt her."

Miss Polly relaxed a little. She thought what a brilliant future it would have meant for Pollyanna. She wondered if Pollyanna were old enough and selfish enough to be tempted by this man's money and position.

"I am very fond of Pollyanna," the man went on. "I am fond of her both for her own sake, and for her mother's. I was ready to give Pollyanna the love that I had held in for twenty-five years."

"*Love.*" With a sinking heart Miss Polly realized that this man had offered Pollyanna what she needed most—and what she herself had not given her. Love. She also realized how dreary her life would be without Pollyanna.

"Well?" she said.

The man smiled sadly. "She would not come," he answered. "She said you had been so good to her. She wanted to stay with you—and she said she *thought* you wanted her to stay."

He did not look toward Miss Polly. He turned his face toward the door. But instantly he heard a swift step at his side, and Miss Polly had put out her hand to grasp his warmly.

"When the specialist comes, and I know anything definite about Pollyanna, you will hear from me," said a trembling voice. "Good-bye—and thank you for coming. Pollyanna will be pleased."

Miss Polly sat with Pollyanna the next day and explained that another doctor would be coming to see her. A joyous light came into Pollyanna's eyes.

"Dr. Chilton! Oh, Aunt Polly, I'd so love to have Dr. Chilton! I'm so glad you do want him!"

Aunt Polly's face turned white, then red, then white again. But she tried to answer cheerily, "No, dear. It's a new doctor—a famous doctor from New York."

Pollyanna's face fell. And Aunt Polly's heart broke. She would do anything—anything but call Dr. Chilton—to please her dear Pollyanna.

And as the days passed, it did indeed seem that Aunt Polly was doing everything (but that) to please her niece. She brought in the cat and the dog to romp with Pollyanna on the bed. ("And she never done *that* before," remarked Nancy.) She dangled the prisms to make the light dance. ("It's as if her heart was just openin' up," Nancy told Old Tom.) And she wore her hair just as Pollyanna had once fixed it—with curls around her forehead. ("Why, she's *pretty*, she is, she is.")

Dr. Meade, from New York, did come to see Pollyanna. He examined her, then turned gravely to Dr. Warren. They left the room to speak.

Everyone said later that it was the cat that did it. Certainly, if Fluffy had not poked at Pollyanna's unlatched door, the door would not have swung open. And if the door had not been open, Pollyanna would not have heard her aunt's words.

In the hall the two doctors, the nurse, and Miss Polly stood talking. In Pollyanna's room Fluffy had just jumped to the bed with a little purr of joy. Then through the open door sounded clearly and sharply Aunt Polly's cry.

"Not that! Doctor, not that! You don't mean the child *will never walk again!*"

It was all confusion then. First, from the bedroom came Pollyanna's terrified "Aunt Polly! Aunt Polly!" Then Miss Polly realized that her words had been heard through the open door. She gave a low little moan, and—for the first time in her life—she fainted.

The nurse stumbled toward the open door. The two doctors stayed in the hall. Dr. Mead had caught Miss Polly, and Dr. Warren stood by helplessly as Pollyanna cried out again.

In Pollyanna's room, the nurse had found a gray cat on the bed purring up at a white-faced, wild-eyed little girl.

"Miss Hunt, please, I want Aunt Polly. I want her right away, quick, please! I want to know what she said just now. I want Aunt Polly to tell me 'tisn't true—'tisn't true!"

The nurse tried to speak, but no words came. Something in her face sent an added terror to Pollyanna's eyes.

"Miss Hunt, it is true! Oh! You don't mean I can't ever—walk again?

"There, there, dear—don't, don't!" choked the nurse. "Perhaps he didn't know. Perhaps he was mistaken. There are lots of things that could happen, you know. All doctors make mistakes sometimes. Don't think any more about it now—please don't, dear."

Pollyanna flung out her arms wildly. "But I can't help thinking about it," she sobbed. "Why, Miss Hunt, how am I to go to school, or to see Mr. Pendleton, or Mrs. Snow?" She sobbed wildly for a moment, then suddenly stopped and looked up.

"Why, Miss Hunt, if I can't walk, how am I ever going to be glad for—*anything*?"

"There, there, dear, just take this medicine," the nurse soothed. "By and by we'll be more rested, and we'll see what can be done then.

Things aren't half as bad as they seem, lots of times, you know."

Pollyanna took the medicine, and sipped the water from the glass in Miss Hunt's hand.

"Father used to say there was always something about everything that might be worse," Pollyanna said. "But I reckon he'd never just heard he couldn't ever walk again. I don't see how there *can* be anything that could be worse—do you?"

But the teary-eyed Miss Hunt could not trust herself to speak just then.

# CHAPTER FOURTEEN

## A Child's Presence

It did not take long for the entire town of Beldingsville to learn that the great New York doctor had said Pollyanna would never walk again. In kitchens and sitting rooms, and over backyard fences, women talked and wept. On street corners the men talked, too, and wept.

To Miss Polly's surprise, the Harrington home began to receive calls—calls from people she knew, and people she did not know: men, women, and children. Some brought books, bunches of flowers, or a food dish. Most wept. All asked about the little injured girl, and all sent her a kind message.

First came Mr. John Pendleton. He came without his crutches.

"I don't need to tell you how shocked I am," he began almost harshly. "But can nothing be done?"

Miss Polly gave a gesture of despair.

"Dr. Mead prescribed certain treatments and medicines that might help... But—he held out almost no hope."

"It seems cruel—never to dance in the sunshine again! My little prism girl!" John Pendleton rose abruptly, though he had just arrived. But at the door he turned.

"I have a message for Pollyanna," he said. "Will you tell her, please, that I have seen Jimmy Bean and—that he's going to be my boy hereafter. Tell her I thought she would be—*glad* to know. I shall adopt him, probably."

Miss Polly stood, silent and amazed, looking after the man who had just left her. Even yet she could scarcely believe what her ears had heard. John Pendleton, wealthy, independent, moody, reputed to be miserly and selfish, to adopt a little boy? And *such* a little boy!

With a somewhat dazed face, Miss Polly went upstairs to Pollyanna's room.

"Pollyanna, I have a message for you from Mr. Pendleton. He has just been here. He says to tell you he has taken Jimmy Bean for his little boy. He said he thought you'd be glad to know it."

Pollyanna's wistful little face flamed into sudden joy.

"Glad? *Glad?* Well, I reckon I am glad! Oh, Aunt Polly, I've so wanted to find a place for Jimmy, and that's such a lovely place! Besides, I'm so glad for Mr. Pendleton, too. You see, now he'll have the child's presence."

"The—what?"

Pollyanna blushed. She had forgotten that she had never told her aunt of Mr. Pendleton's wish to adopt her. And certainly she would not want to tell her now that she had ever thought for a minute of leaving her—this dear Aunt Polly!

"The child's presence," stammered Pollyanna hastily. "Mr. Pendleton told me once, you see, that only a woman's hand and heart or a child's presence could make a home. And now he's got it—the child's presence."

"Oh, I see," said Miss Polly very gently. She did see, more than Pollyanna realized. Her eyes were stinging with sudden tears for this caring child.

Pollyanna tried to change the subject.

"Dr. Chilton says so, too—that it takes a woman's hand and heart, or a child's presence, to make a home, you know," she remarked.

Miss Polly turned with a start.

"*Dr. Chilton*! How do you know—that?"

"He told me so."

Miss Polly did not answer. Her eyes were out the window.

"So I asked him why he didn't get 'em— a woman's hand and heart, and have a home."

"Pollyanna!" Miss Polly had turned sharply. Her cheeks showed a sudden color.

"Well, I did. He looked so—so sorrowful."

"What did he—say?" Miss Polly asked the question as if in spite of some force within her that was urging her not to ask it.

"He didn't say anything for a minute. Then he said very low that you couldn't always get 'em for the asking."

There was a brief silence. Miss Polly had turned again to the window. Her cheeks were quite pink.

Pollyanna sighed.

"He wants one, anyhow, I know, and I wish he could have one."

"Why, Pollyanna, *how* do you know?"

"Because, afterwards, on another day, he said that he'd give all the world if he did have one woman's hand and heart. Why, Aunt Polly, what's the matter?" Aunt Polly had risen hurriedly and gone to the window.

"Nothing, dear. I was changing the position of this prism," said Aunt Polly, whose whole face now was aflame.

# CHAPTER FIFTEEN

## *The Game and Its Players*

It was not long after John Pendleton's visit that Milly Snow called one afternoon. She blushed and looked very embarrassed when Miss Polly entered the room.

"I—I c-came to inquire for the—the little girl," she stammered.

"You are very kind. She is about the same. How is your mother?" asked Miss Polly wearily.

"That is what I came to tell Pollyanna," the girl said nervously. "After all she's done for mother—teaching her to play the game and all. We heard how now she couldn't play it herself. We thought if she could only know what she *had* done for us,

that it would *help*. She could be glad—that is, a little glad—" Milly stopped and waited for Miss Polly to speak.

"I don't think I quite understand, Milly. Just what is it that you want me to tell my niece?"

"You know nothing was ever right before for Mother. But now she lets me keep the shades up, and she takes interest in things. And she's actually begun to knit little things for fairs and hospitals. She's so *glad* to think she can do it.

"That was all Miss Pollyanna's doings," Milly went on. "She told Mother to be glad she had her hands and arms. That made Mother wonder why she didn't *do* something with her hands and arms. So she began to knit. We want you to please tell Miss Pollyanna that we understand it's all because of her. Maybe if she knew it, it would make her a little glad that she knew us. You'll tell her?"

These visits of John Pendleton and Milly Snow were only the first of many.

One day there was the Widow Tarbell.

"I'm a stranger to you, of course," she began at once. "But I'm not a stranger to your little niece, Pollyanna. I've been at the hotel all summer, and every day I've taken long walks for my health.

It was on these walks that I've met your niece. She's such a dear little girl! Her bright face and cheery ways reminded me of my own little girl that I lost years ago. I was so shocked to hear of the accident. The dear child! Will you just tell her that Mrs. Tarbell is glad now? I know it sounds odd, and you don't understand. But—if you'll pardon me, I'd rather not explain. Your niece will know just what I mean. Thank you, and pardon me, please, if I seem rude," she begged, as she left.

Miss Polly, by now confused, hurried upstairs to Pollyanna's room.

"Pollyanna, do you know a Mrs. Tarbell?"

"Oh, yes. I love Mrs. Tarbell. She's sick, and awfully sad, and she's at the hotel, and takes long walks. We go together. I mean—we used to." Pollyanna's voice broke, and two big tears rolled down her cheeks.

Miss Polly cleared her throat hurriedly.

"We'll, she's just been here, dear. She left a message for you—but she wouldn't tell me what it meant. She said to tell you that she's glad now."

Pollyanna clapped her hands softly.

"Did she say that—really? Oh, I'm so glad!"

"But, Pollyanna, what did she mean?"

"Why, it's the game, and—" Pollyanna stopped short, her fingers to her lips.

"What game?"

"N-nothing much, Aunt Polly. That is, I can't tell it unless I tell other things that I'm not to speak of."

Miss Polly wanted to question her niece further, but the distress on the little girl's face stopped the words before they were uttered.

Yet another visitor, a Mrs. Benton, showed up in her usual widow's black—but with a big blue bow at her throat.

"Will you tell the little girl I'm playing the game—and I've put on a bit of color?" she asked.

The door had scarcely closed behind her before Miss Polly went up to Nancy in the kitchen.

"Nancy, *will* you tell me what this 'game' is that the whole town seems to be babbling about? And what, please, has my niece to do with it?"

To Miss Polly's surprise and dismay, Nancy burst into tears.

"It means that ever since last June that blessed child has been makin' the whole town glad, an' now they're tryin' to make her a little glad, too. It's the game."

Miss Polly actually stamped her foot.

"There you go like all the rest. What game?"

"It's a game Miss Pollyanna's father learned her to play. She got a pair of crutches once when she was wantin' a doll. She cried like any child would. Her father told her that there was always somethin' to be glad about, an' that she could be glad about them crutches."

"Glad for *crutches*!" Miss Polly choked back a sob. She was thinking of the helpless little legs on the bed upstairs.

"Yes'm. He told her she could be glad 'cause she *didn't need 'em*. And after that he made a regular game of finding somethin' in everythin' to be glad about. And they called it the 'jest bein' glad' game. She's played it ever since."

"But why has she made such a mystery of it, when I asked her?"

Nancy hesitated.

"Beggin' yer pardon, ma'am, you told her not to speak of her father. She couldn't tell ye. 'Twas her father's game, ye see."

Miss Polly bit her lip.

"She wanted to tell ye, first off," Nancy went on, a little nervously. "She wanted somebody to play it with, ye know. That's why I begun it, so she could have someone."

"And these others?" Miss Polly's voice shook.

"Oh, almost everybody knows it now. Anyhow, I hear of it everywhere I go. Ye see, she's always wanted everybody to play the game with her."

"Well, I know somebody who'll play it now," choked Miss Polly, as she turned and sped through the kitchen doorway.

A little later, in Pollyanna's room, the nurse left Miss Polly and Pollyanna alone together.

"You've had another caller today, my dear," said Miss Polly quietly. "Do you remember Mrs. Benton? She came with a bright blue bow on."

Pollyanna smiled through tear-wet eyes.

"Did she? Did she, really? Oh, I am so glad!"

"Yes, she said she hoped you'd be. That's why she told you, to make you—*glad*, Pollyanna."

"Why, Aunt Polly, you spoke just as if you knew. *Do* you know about the game?"

"Yes, dear. Nancy told me. I think it's a beautiful game, and I'm going to play it now with you. Why, Pollyanna, I think all the town is wonderfully happier because one little girl taught people a new game."

Pollyanna clapped her hands. Then, suddenly, a wonderful light shone in her face.

"Why, Aunt Polly, there *is* something I can be glad about, after all. I can be glad I've *had* my legs, anyway—else I couldn't have done that!"

# CHAPTER SIXTEEN

# *Through an Open Window*

One by one the short winter days came and went. But they were not short to Pollyanna. They were long, and sometimes full of pain. But the little girl found ways to be cheerful. How could she not, with Aunt Polly playing the game now? Aunt Polly found *so* many things to be glad about! And, like Mrs. Snow, Pollyanna knitted wonderful things out of bright colored strings. She was glad she had her hands and arms, anyway.

Pollyanna saw people now, and always there were loving messages from those she could not see. They brought her something to think about—and Pollyanna needed new things to think about.

Once she had seen John Pendleton, and twice she had seen Jimmy Bean. John Pendleton had told her what a fine boy Jimmy was, and how well he was doing. Jimmy had told her what a first-rate home he had, and what bang-up "folks" Mr. Pendleton made. Both had said that it was all because of her.

The winter passed and spring came, but Pollyanna's treatment brought little change. There seemed every reason to believe that Pollyanna would never walk again.

Mr. John Pendleton, somewhat to his surprise, received a call one Saturday morning from Dr. Thomas Chilton.

"Pendleton," said the doctor, "I've come to you because you know about my... er... well, feelings for Miss Polly Harrington."

John Pendleton was taken aback. He did know that Miss Polly and Chilton had once been in love, but they had not talked of it for fifteen years.

"Pendleton, I want to see that child. I want to examine her. I *must* make an examination."

"Well—can't you?"

"*Can't* I? Pendleton, you know very well I have not been inside that door for over fifteen years.

Polly Harrington told me that the next time she *asked* me to enter it, I would know she was begging my pardon. It would mean everything would be as before—that she'd marry me. Perhaps you see her calling me now—but I don't!"

"If you're so anxious, couldn't you swallow your pride and forget the quarrel?"

"Forget the quarrel!" interrupted the doctor. "I'm not talking of that kind of pride. This is a case of sickness, and I'm a doctor. I can't butt in and say, 'Here, take me!' can I?"

"Chilton, what was the quarrel?"

"What's any lovers' quarrel after it's over?" Chilton snarled, pacing the room. "Never mind the quarrel! Pendleton, I must see that child. It may mean life or death. It will mean, nine chances out of ten, that Pollyanna Whittier will walk again!"

The words were spoken clearly, and they were spoken just as Dr. Chilton reached the open window near John Pendleton's chair. So it happened that a small boy kneeling beneath the window outside heard them.

Little Jimmy Bean sat up with ears and eyes wide open.

"Walk? Pollyanna?" John Pendleton was saying. "What do you mean?"

"I mean that her case is very much like one that a college friend of mine has just helped. For years he's been making this sort of thing a special study. I've kept in touch with him, and studied, too. I want to *see* the girl! But how can I, without a direct request from her aunt?"

"She must be made to ask you!"

"How?"

"I don't know."

Outside the window, Jimmy Bean stirred suddenly. Up to now, he had scarcely breathed.

"Well, by Jinks, *I* know how! I'll do it!" he whispered excitedly.

He crept around the corner of the house. Then he ran with all his might down Pendleton Hill to Miss Polly Harrington's house.

"It's Jimmy Bean. He wants to see ye, ma'am," announced Nancy in the doorway.

"Me?" asked Miss Polly, plainly surprised.

"Yes'm. He said it was you he wanted."

In the sitting room she found a round-eyed, flushed-faced boy, who began to speak at once.

"Ma'am, I suppose it's dreadful—what I'm doin', an' what I'm sayin', but I can't help it. It's for Pollyanna, an' that's why I come to tell ye that it's only pride that's keepin' Pollyanna from walkin'. I knew you *would* ask Dr. Chilton here if you understood."

"What? Jimmy, what are you talking about? Begin at the beginning, and be sure I understand each thing as you go. Don't plunge into the middle of it."

"Well, to begin with, Dr. Chilton come to see Mr. Pendleton, an' they talked in the library," Jimmy said. "Do you understand that?"

"Yes, Jimmy," Miss Polly said faintly.

"Well, the window was open, and I was weedin' the flowerbed under it. I heard 'em talk. Dr. Chilton knows some doctor that can cure Pollyanna, but he can't be sure till he *sees* her. But he told Mr. Pendleton that you wouldn't let him."

Miss Polly's face turned very red.

"But, Jimmy, I can't—I couldn't! That is, I didn't know!"

"Yes, an' I come to tell ye, so you *would* know," said Jimmy eagerly. "They said that you wouldn't let Dr. Chilton come. An' Dr. Chilton couldn't come himself, without you asked him, on account of pride. An' they was wishin' somebody could make you understand, only they didn't know who could. An' I was outside the window, an' I says to myself right away, 'By Jinks, I'll do it!' An' I come—an' have I made ye understand?"

Miss Polly turned her head from side to side. Jimmy, watching her with anxious eyes, thought she was going to cry. But she did not cry. After a minute she said brokenly, "Yes, Jimmy. I'll let Dr. Chilton see her. Now run home, Jimmy— quick! I've got to speak to Dr. Warren about bringing Dr. Chilton in. He's upstairs now. I saw him drive in a few minutes ago."

The next time Dr. Warren entered Pollyanna's room, a tall, broad-shouldered man followed close behind him.

"Dr. Chilton! Oh, Dr. Chilton, how glad I am to see *you*!" cried Pollyanna. And at the joy in her voice, more than one pair of eyes in the room brimmed with tears.

"It is all right, my dear, don't worry," soothed Miss Polly. "I told Dr. Chilton that I want him to look you over with Dr. Warren."

"Oh, then you asked him to come," murmured Pollyanna contentedly.

"Yes, dear, I asked him. That is—" And then Miss Polly's eyes met Dr. Chilton's eyes. They were filled with adoring happiness. With very pink cheeks, Miss Polly turned and left the room.

Over at the window the nurse and Dr. Warren were talking. Dr. Chilton smiled and held out both his hands to Pollyanna.

"Little girl, one of the very gladdest jobs you ever did has been done today," he said in a voice shaken with emotion.

At twilight, a wonderfully different Aunt Polly crept to Pollyanna's bedside. The nurse was at supper. They had the room to themselves.

"Pollyanna, dear, I'm going to tell *you* first of all. Someday Dr. Chilton will be your uncle. We're to be married. And *you* have made it all happen. Oh, Pollyanna, I'm so—glad!—darling!"

Pollyanna began to clap her hands.

"Oh, Aunt Polly, *you* were the woman's hand and heart he wanted so long ago! I knew you were! And that's what he meant by saying I'd done the gladdest job of all today. Why, Aunt Polly, I think I'm so glad that I don't mind even my legs, now!"

Aunt Polly swallowed a sob.

"Perhaps, someday, dear—" But Aunt Polly did not dare to tell yet the great hope that Dr. Chilton had put into her heart. She did say this, which was quite wonderful to Pollyanna's mind:

"Pollyanna, next week you're going to take a journey. On a nice comfortable little bed, you're going to be carried to a great doctor. He has a big house many miles from here for people with injured legs. He's a dear friend of Dr. Chilton's, and we're going to see what he can do for you!"

# CHAPTER SEVENTEEN

# A Letter from Pollyanna

*Dear Aunt Polly and Uncle Tom,*

*Oh, I can—I can—I can walk! I did today all the way from my bed to the window! It was six steps. My, how good it was to be on legs again!*

*All the doctors stood around and smiled, and all the nurses cried. A lady who walked last week peeked into the door. Another one, who hopes she can walk next month, was invited to the party. She lay on my nurse's bed and clapped her hands. Even Tilly, who washes the floor, looked through the patio window. She called me 'Honey child' when she wasn't crying too much to call me anything.*

*I don't see why they cried. I wanted to sing and shout and yell! Oh—oh—oh! Just think, I can walk—walk—walk! Now I don't mind being here almost ten months. And I didn't miss the wedding, anyhow. Wasn't that just like you, Aunt Polly, to come here and get married right beside my bed, so I could see you. You always do think of the gladdest things!*

*Pretty soon, they say, I shall go home. I wish I could walk all the way there. I do. I don't think I shall ever want to ride anywhere any more. It will be so good just to walk. Oh, I'm so glad! I'm glad for everything. Why, I'm glad now I lost my legs for a while. For you never, never know how perfectly lovely legs are till you haven't got them—legs that go, I mean. I'm going to walk eight steps tomorrow.*

*With heaps of love to everybody,*
*—Pollyanna*


## THE END

## ELEANOR H. PORTER

Eleanor Hodgman was born on December 19, 1868, in Littleton, New Hampshire. She did not spend much time in a formal school, since her family believed exploring the outdoors would teach her more.

She loved music and studied singing at the New England Conservatory of Music in Boston. She became a popular singer in concerts and church choirs in the area, and continued singing after she married John L. Porter, a businessman, in 1892.

In 1901, Eleanor became more interested in writing than in singing. She wrote short stories for magazines and newspapers. Her first popular book was *Miss Billy* in 1911, which had two sequels, followed by *Pollyanna* in 1913, and *Pollyanna Grows Up* in 1915. *Pollyanna* was a bestseller and inspired "glad clubs" all over the country and world. The book has also been made into a play and several movies.

Eleanor continued to write for the rest of her life, sometimes using the pen name of Eleanor Stuart. She died on May 21, 1920, in Cambridge, Massachusetts.

# REBECCA OF
# SUNNYBROOK
# FARM

KATE DOUGLAS WIGGIN

CONDENSED AND ADAPTED BY
LOUISE COLLN

ILLUSTRATED BY
RUTH PALMER

# CONTENTS

Characters................................................. 382

1. Rebecca Randall .................................. 387

2. The Brick House................................. 399

3. Sunday Letters .................................. 413

4. Sunshine in a Shady Place .................................. 417

5. A Pink Dress and a Dark Storm ........................ 427

6. A Rainbow Bridge ................................ 439

7. Rebecca's Punishment ........................ 451

8. Mr. Aladdin ........................................ 459

9. The Banquet Lamp .............................. 469

10. Seasons of Change .............................. 483

11. Rebecca Represents the Family ........................ 489

12. School in Wareham .............................. 499

13. A Heart in Bloom ............................ 505

14. Aladdin Grants Some Wishes.................... 515

15. The Gates of Childhood........................ 525

16. Leaving Childhood Behind .................... 535

17. "Good-bye, Sunnybrook!" .................... 547

18. Aunt Miranda's Apology ...................... 557

About the Author .............................. 565

REBECCA ROWENA RANDALL — a young girl who lives with her aunts so she can go to school and help her family

LORENZO DE MEDICI RANDALL — Rebecca's happy, talented father who died when Rebecca was young

AURELIA SAWYER RANDALL — Rebecca's hardworking mother with seven children

HANNAH — Rebecca's sensible, patient older sister, who marries Will Melville

JOHN, JENNY, MARK, FANNY, AND MIRA — the younger brothers and sisters that Hannah and Rebecca help to raise

THE COBBS — the stagecoach driver and his wife ("Uncle Jerry and Aunt Sarah") who always have time for Rebecca

AUNT MIRANDA SAWYER — Rebecca's strict aunt – set in her ways, very neat and clean

# CHARACTERS

AUNT JANE SAWYER — Rebecca's kind aunt, who helps Rebecca find ways to get along with Aunt Miranda

EMMA JANE PERKINS — Rebecca's most loyal and best friend

THE SIMPSON FAMILY — a large family in Riverboro, going through hard times

MISS DEARBORN — the teacher at the Riverboro school

ADAM LADD — the young gentleman who is "Mr. Aladdin" to Rebecca

REV. BURCH — a missionary who stays with his family overnight at the "brick house"

HULDAH MESERVE — a stylish fellow student at Wareham Academy

MISS MAXWELL — the teacher at Wareham Academy, who helps Rebecca to travel and write

# Rebecca of
# Sunnybrook Farm

# CHAPTER ONE

## *Rebecca Randall*

The old stagecoach was rumbling along the dusty Maine road. The day was warm, though it was the middle of May. Mr. Jeremiah Cobb had driven this mail route from Maplewood to Riverboro many times. He settled back with his hat pulled low.

There was only one passenger in the coach. It was a small dark-haired person in a tan dress. She, too, was trying to settle into the ride. But she was so slender and her dress was so starched that she kept sliding on the leather cushions. She tried to brace herself with her small, gloved hands. But whenever the wheels sank down into a rut,

or jolted over a stone, she bounced up into the air and down again. Each time, she pushed back her funny straw hat and tried to get settled again. Every now and then, she picked up her small pink parasol and bouquet of lilacs—or she peeked into a little bead purse. Mr. Cobb did not even know that his passenger was having such a bouncy, slippery ride.

A woman at the Maplewood station had asked Mr. Cobb to drive her little girl to Riverboro. The mother helped the child into the stagecoach, loaded a trunk, and then paid Mr. Cobb.

"Do you know Miranda and Jane Sawyer?" she asked. "They live in the brick house in Riverboro."

"Lord bless your soul!" replied Mr. Cobb. "I know 'em well!"

"Well, they are my sisters. I am Aurelia Randall, and this is my daughter, Rebecca. She is going to stay with them. They know she's coming. Will you keep an eye on her, please? You see, she's kind of excited… We've had a long trip. Yesterday we came on the train from the town of Temperance. We slept at my Cousin Ann's house, and then drove her buggy here—eight miles it is—all this morning. Well, good-bye, Rebecca.

Try not to get into any mischief. And sit quiet, so you'll look neat and nice when you get there. Don't be any trouble to Mr. Cobb."

"Good-bye, Mother. And don't worry. After all, I *have* traveled before."

The woman chuckled. "She's been to Wareham and stayed overnight. That isn't much traveling!"

"It *was traveling*, Mother," said the child eagerly. "It was leaving the farm, and packing a lunch basket, and riding in a buggy, and then on a train. And we carried our nightgowns!"

"Rebecca!" said the mother. "Haven't I told you before that you shouldn't talk of nightgowns and stockings and—things like that?"

"I know, Mother, I know. I just meant—"

Mr. Cobb slapped the reins, and the horses started on down the road.

"—I just meant—it really *is* traveling when—" Rebecca put her head out the window and yelled back to her mother, "when you carry a nightgown!"

Mrs. Randall watched the stagecoach rumble down the road in a cloud of dust.

"Mirandy will have her hands full, I guess," she said to herself. "But I think my sisters will be the making of Rebecca."

All this had been half an hour ago, and Mr. Cobb had forgotten about his passenger. Then, suddenly, he heard a small voice above the noise of the wheels. At first he thought it was a cricket, a tree toad, or a bird. He turned his head over his shoulder and saw a small shape hanging out of the window. It was the child! Her long black braid of hair was flying in the air. With one hand she held her hat. With the other, she was trying to poke at him with her pink parasol.

"Please let me speak!" she called.

Mr. Cobb pulled lightly on the reins to slow up the horses.

"Does it cost any more to ride up there with you?" she asked. "It's so slippery that I'm sliding around here. I'm almost black and blue. And the windows are so small, I can't see much outside."

"You can come up if you want to," Mr. Cobb said cheerfully. "There's no extra charge." He stopped the horses and helped her up to the seat beside him.

"Oh! This is better! I am a real passenger now! It's a good day, isn't it?" said the girl.

"Too hot, mostly. Why don't you put up your little parasol?"

"Oh dear, no!" she said. "I never put it up when the sun shines. Pink fades awfully, you know. I only carry it to church on Sundays—if it's cloudy. It's the dearest thing in life to me. Did you notice the double ruffle and ivory handle?"

Mr. Cobb took his first good look at the passenger perched by his side. The girl stared back with friendly curiosity. She looked to be about ten or eleven, but she seemed small for her age. Her plain little face was brown and thin. There was nothing unusual, really, about her— but those eyes! They lit up her face and glowed like two stars. They made him think of a verse from the Bible about faith—*the substance of things hoped for, the evidence of things not seen.* They almost seemed to look right through him to something deeper. "Why, those eyes," Mr. Cobb later told his wife, "could knock a person galley-west!"

"The ivory handle has scratches, you see," Rebecca went on. "That's because Fanny chewed it in church when I wasn't looking."

"Is Fanny your sister?"

"She's one of them."

"How many are there of you?"

"Seven. There's poetry written about seven children—*Quick was the little Maid's reply, O master, we are seven!* Mr. Wordsworth wrote it. He was a poet. He lived in England. I learned those lines in school. Hannah is the oldest, I come next, then John, then Jenny, then Mark, then Fanny, then Mira. Mira is named after Aunt Miranda. We're all named after someone. My name is taken out of the book *Ivanhoe*. My father knew all the best books, you see. His name was Lorenzo— Lorenzo de Medici Randall. Isn't that a fine name? Mother says we must always stand up for Father, because it was only bad luck that made us poor. Mira was born the day Father died. She's three now, and Mother says we're stopping at seven. We'll all have a lovely time when we're all grown up and the farm mortgage is paid off."

Mr. Cobb smiled. "Maybe we'd best share our names since we're goin' to be ridin' together. I'm Jeremiah Cobb, but most folks call me Jerry."

"My name is Rebecca Rowena Randall. I'm going to live with my Aunt Miranda and Aunt Jane Sawyer in the brick house in Riverboro."

"I know them well," replied Jerry. "Your farm back home ain't the old Hobbs place, is it?"

"No, it's just Randall's Farm. At least that's what Mother calls it. I call it Sunnybrook Farm. It matters what you name a place, don't you think? It has a chattering little brook with a white sandy bottom and lots of shiny pebbles. Whenever there's a bit of sunshine, the brook catches it. It's always full of sparkles the livelong day."

Mr. Cobb began to realize what an unusual little person Rebecca was. "I guess you're in school and it ain't no trouble for you to learn your lessons, is it?"

"Not much. The trouble is to get the shoes to *go* to school. I've read lots of books, though. Any I can get! Have you read *Cinderella*, or *The Yellow Dwarf*, or *The Enchanted Frog*, or *The Fair One with Golden Locks*? I even try the hard ones like *David Copperfield*! I'll be going to school when I'm living with Aunt Miranda. And in two years I'm going to the Academy at Wareham. Mother says it ought to be the making of me!"

# CHAPTER TWO

## *The Brick House*

"'Tain't far, now," Mr. Cobb told Rebecca when he saw the village of Riverboro in the distance. "I live 'bout half a mile beyond the brick house myself. You come see me—and ride with me while I deliver papers. Now you watch me heave this newspaper right onto Miss Brown's doorstep."

Mr. Cobb flung a packet and *pfft!* it landed on the front mat.

"Oh, how splendid!" cried Rebecca. "Just like the knife thrower Mark saw at the circus."

"Well, if your Aunt Mirandy will let you, I'll take you down to Milltown some day this summer when the stagecoach ain't full."

Rebecca was thrilled from her new shoes up—up to the straw hat and down the black braid. "Oh, to think I could see Milltown!" she whispered. But then her face changed. "I didn't think I was going to be afraid," she said quietly, "but I guess I am, just a little, when you say it's coming so near. Aunt Miranda wanted Hannah to come instead of me, but mother couldn't spare her. Hannah takes hold of housework better than I do."

"Would you go back?" asked Mr. Cobb.

She flashed him a brave look. "I'd *never* go back! I might be afraid, but I'd be ashamed to run. But I do think I better get back into the stagecoach. That's where Mother put me, and that's where a lady should sit. Would you please stop a minute, Mr. Cobb, and let me change?"

Mr. Cobb smiled and stopped the horses. He lifted the excited little girl down, helped her in, and put the lilacs and pink parasol beside her.

"We've had a great trip," he said, "and we've gotten to be friends, haven't we? You won't forget about Milltown?"

"Never!" she exclaimed. "And you're sure you won't either?"

"Never! Cross my heart!" vowed Mr. Cobb.

The stagecoach rumbled down the village street between the green maples. Anyone who looked from their windows would have seen a little elf in a faded brown dress clutching a great bouquet in one hand and a pink parasol in the other. And anyone who could look closely might have seen two pale cheeks, and a mist of tears swimming in two dark eyes.

Rebecca's journey had ended.

"There's the stage turning into the Sawyer girls' yard," said Mrs. Perkins to her husband. "That must be the niece from up Temperance way. She'll be good company for our Emma Jane. Why, she looks dark as an Indian! Must be her Spanish blood. They used to say that one of the Randalls married a Spanish woman. Well, I don't know as that Spanish blood didn't give her somethin' special— she looks like an up-and-comin' child."

The stage came to the side door of the brick house. There stood two proper ladies—Aunt Miranda and Aunt Jane. Rebecca got out carefully. She put the bunch of faded flowers in her Aunt Miranda's hand.

Aunt Miranda greeted her stiffly. "You needn't have bothered to bring flowers. The garden's always full of 'em here when it comes time."

Aunt Jane kissed Rebecca. "Put the trunk in the entry, Jeremiah, and we'll get it carried upstairs this afternoon," she said.

"Well, g'bye, Rebecca," said Mr. Cobb. "Good day, Mirandy 'n' Jane. You've got a lively little girl there. I guess she'll be first-rate company."

Miss Miranda shuddered. "We're not much used to noise, Jane and me," she remarked.

They had been called the Sawyer girls when Miranda, Jane, and Aurelia were teenagers in the village. Miranda and Jane, spinsters of fifty and sixty, were still called the Sawyer girls. Miranda Sawyer was thrifty, hardworking, and very cold of heart. Jane was softer and gentler. It was Jane who had gone to nurse wounded soldiers in the War Between the States—after her fiancé had died in battle. She had not left Riverboro since.

Aurelia, Rebecca's mother, was the only one who had married. It was a "romantic marriage," she said. "A mighty poor one," her sisters said. Aurelia had a modest share of the Sawyer money. But Rebecca's father had lost it long before they bought the rundown Sunnybrook Farm. The handsome Lorenzo de Medici Randall was not gifted with making money. Farming was not in his soul. Instead, he taught weekly singing school, played violin, and "called off" at village dances.

Rebecca, of all the Randall children, was most like her father. She had his zest for life and music and his sense of humor. She sang alto by ear, danced without being taught, played the church organ. And she loved books, especially classics.

She was a thing of fire and spirit—a plucky girl. And she could be headstrong. She was not as patient as her older sister, Hannah. And not as steady as John. Aurelia thought she was too skittish and dreamy—and not responsible. Like her sisters, Miranda and Jane, Aurelia admired plain, everyday common sense. Rebecca did not seem to have much of this. And so Miranda and Jane were not looking forward to Rebecca's arrival—especially Miranda.

It had been several years since Miranda and Jane Sawyer had visited Sunnybrook Farm. They remembered Rebecca as wild, and Hannah as a quiet, dependable child. That is the reason her aunts had invited Hannah to Riverboro to live with them. The Riverboro schools would be better for her education. So, when they got their sister's letter saying she was sending Rebecca, they were shocked. Instead of down-to-earth Hannah, here was this black-haired gypsy, with eyes as big as cartwheels. How would they deal with her?

"I'll take you up and show you your room, Rebecca," Miss Miranda said. "Shut the door tight behind you. We don't want flies. Wipe your feet. Hang your hat and cape in the entry there as you go past. Lay your parasol in the entry closet."

"Do you mind if I keep them in my room, please? It always seems safer."

"There ain't any thieves around. Come along. Remember to always go up the back way. We don't use the front stairs on account of the carpet. Now look to your right and go in. When you've washed your face and hands and brushed your hair, you can come down. By and by we'll unpack your trunk and get you settled before supper."

Miranda stood studying the child. "Ain't you got your dress on backwards?" she said.

Rebecca looked at the row of buttons running down her chest. "Backwards? Oh, I see! No, that's all right. We're always buttoned up the front at our house. With seven children, Mother can't button and unbutton us all, you know, so this way we can do the buttons ourselves!"

Miranda frowned and said nothing as she closed the door.

Rebecca stood perfectly still in the center of the room and looked about her. There was a square of oilcloth in front of each piece of furniture. A rag rug lay beside the single bed, which was covered with a fringed white spread. Everything was as neat as wax. Far nicer than her room at the farm! It was a north-facing room. The long, narrow window looked out on the back buildings and the barn.

Rebecca didn't feel at all tired. But she did have a feeling she couldn't quite understand— part fear, part excitement. She stood her parasol in the corner. Then, in a rush of emotion, she tore off her hat, flung herself into the middle of the bed, and pulled the cover over her head.

In a moment the door opened and Miss Miranda entered without knocking.

"*Rebecca!*" she cried sternly.

A dark ruffled head and two frightened eyes appeared above the cover.

"What are you layin' on your good bed in the daytime for? You're messin' up the feathers, and dirtyin' the pillows with your dusty boots!"

Rebecca rose guiltily, knowing that she could not explain.

"I'm sorry, Aunt Miranda. Something came over me. I don't know what."

"Well, if it comes over you again very soon we'll have to find out what it is. Spread your bed up smooth this minute."

# CHAPTER THREE

## Sunday Letters

*Dear Mother,*

*I am safely here. My dress didn't get too rumpled. I like Mr. Cobb very much. He throws newspapers strate to the doors. The brick house looks just the same as you have told us. The parler is splendid and gives you creeps and chills when you look in the door. The furnature is ellergant too, and all the rooms, but there are no good sitting-down places exsept in the kitchen. Aunt M. is not happy with me at all, but Aunt J. is kinder to me. She does not hate me as bad as Aunt M. does. Aunt J. gave me a dictionary to look up hard words in. That takes a good deal of time.*

*I am glad people can talk without stopping to spell. It is much eesier to talk than write and much more fun. Tell Mark he can have my paint box. I hope Hannah and John do not get tired doing my chores.*

 *Your afectionate friend*
 *Rebecca*

*p.s. Please give this poetry I wrote to John because he likes poetry even when it is not very good.*

## SUNDAY THOUGHTS
by Rebecca Rowena Randall

This house is dark and dull and drear
No light doth shine from far or near
 'Tis like a tomb.

My guardian angel is asleep
At least he doth no vigil keep
 But far doth roam.

Then give me back my lonely farm
Where none alive did wish me harm,
 Dear childhood home!

*Dear Mother,*

*I am not happy this morning. Aunt M. was very cross and unfealing to me. Have I only been here a week? I wish Hannah had come instead of me for it was Hannah that they wanted and she is better than I am.*

*School is pretty good. I am smarter than Emma Jane Perkins and the other girls but not so smart as two boys. I am in the Sixth Reader. But just because I cannot say the Multiplication Table, Miss Dearborn threttens to put me in the baby class with the Simpson twins. I read with Dick Carter and Living Perkins, who are studying for the academy. Miss Dearborn teaches me grammer after the others have gone home.*

*I sew on brown gingham dresses every afternoon while Emma Jane and the Simpsons are playing. I can play from half past four to supper and after supper a little bit and Saturday afternoons. It is going to be a good year for apples and hay so you and John will be glad we can pay a little more of the morgage on the farm. Miss Dearborn asked us what is the object of edducation and I said the object of mine was to help pay off the morgage. She told Aunt M. and*

*I had to sew extra for punishment because she says a morgage is a disgrace like stealing or smallpox and it will be all over town that we owe money on our farm.*

*Sometimes I feer I cannot bare this life.*
*Your afectionate friend*
*Rebecca.*

*Dear John,*
*You remember when we tide the new dog in the barn how he bit the rope and howled? I am just like him only the brick house is the barn and I can not bite Aunt M. because I must be grateful and edducation is going to be the making of me and help you pay off the morgage when we grow up.*
*Your loving*
*Becky*

# CHAPTER FOUR

## Sunshine in a Shady Place

Rebecca had started school right away in Riverboro, with only one month left in the school year. The little schoolhouse had a flagpole on top and stood on the crest of a hill. There were rolling fields and pine woods around it, and the river sparkled in the distance. But it was bare and ugly inside. There was an old black stove, a map of the United States, and two blackboards. On a corner shelf was a tin pail of drinking water with a long-handled dipper.

Miss Dearborn, the teacher, had a desk and chair on a platform. The twenty students sat on hard benches behind wooden desks.

Rebecca walked to school every morning. She loved this part of the day. She clasped her books in one hand, and her lunch pail swung from the other. She had blissful thoughts of the two soda biscuits spread with butter and syrup, the baked cup-custard, the doughnut, and the square of hard gingerbread in her lunch.

When the weather was fair, Rebecca and her new best friend, Emma Jane Perkins, took a short cut through the woods. They turned off the main road, crept through Uncle Josh Woodman's gate, and waved away Mrs. Carter's cows. They went down a well-worn path running through buttercups and sweet fern. They jumped from stone to stone across a brook. They went through the woods, climbed the steps of a wooden stile to get over another fence, went through a grassy meadow, slid under another gate, and came out into the road again.

At the last gate the two girls were met by some of the Simpson children. The Simpsons were poor and lived in a bleak house. Rebecca sympathized with the Simpsons. There were so many of them. They were covered in patches, just like her own family at Sunnybrook Farm.

It was fortunate that Rebecca had her books and her new friends, or she would have been unhappy that first summer after school ended. She made a great effort to please her grim and difficult Aunt Miranda. But her aunt's searching eyes, sharp voice, hard knotty fingers, thin straight lips, and long silences made it hard.

Rebecca irritated her aunt with every breath she drew. She forgot and used the front stairs because it was the shortest way to her bedroom. She left the dipper on the kitchen shelf instead of hanging it up over the pail. She sat in the chair the cat liked best. She was willing to go on errands, but often forgot what she was sent for. She left the screen doors open, and flies came in.

Aunt Jane was sunshine in a shady place to Rebecca. With her quiet voice and her kind eyes, she made Rebecca's life easier those first difficult weeks. Oh, those "brick house ways" were so hard to learn for this spirited little stranger!

Rebecca needed Aunt Jane's understanding as she struggled to sew dresses from endless yards of brown gingham. She broke the thread, pricked her finger, could not match the checks, and puckered the seams.

After Rebecca had been in Riverboro for several months—and after she had made several brown gingham dresses—she asked her Aunt Miranda if she might have another color for the next dress.

"I don't approve of children being rigged out in fancy colors, but I'll see what your Aunt Jane thinks," was the sharp reply.

"I think it would be all right to let Rebecca have one pink and one blue gingham," said Jane. "A child gets tired of sewing on one color. It's only natural she should long for a change. Besides, she'd look like a charity child always wearing the same brown. And brown looks dreadful on her!"

And so pink and blue gingham were ordered.

Rebecca worked her hardest on the pink dress. One afternoon, when she had nearly finished, Aunt Jane promised to make a pretty white trim for it. And she gave Rebecca permission to go and play with Emma Jane and Alice Robinson.

Rebecca leaped off the porch. She and her friends had several favorite places to play. The Simpsons had the most fascinating front yard in the village. It was filled with junk like old sleighs, broken couches, beds without headboards—

and never the same stuff on any two days. Mr. Abner Simpson spent little time with his family. He had a bad habit of trading off things belonging to his neighbors. So after every trade, he generally spent some time in jail. Mrs. Simpson took in washing and the town helped in the feeding and clothing of the children.

Next to the Simpson yard there was a velvety stretch of ground beside a group of trees in the Sawyer pasture. The children brought pieces of wood from the sawmill to build houses there. They stored all their treasures in soapboxes: wee baskets and plates and cups, bits of broken china for parties, and dolls. They played out stories with their dolls in the playhouses—school, weddings, funerals, and tales from their books.

This afternoon they built a tall, square house around Rebecca. She was a romantic royal prisoner leaning against the bars of her prison. It was a wonderful experience standing inside the building with Emma Jane's apron wound about her hair, pretending to be a sad princess.

"I hate to have to take it down," said Alice, when it was time to go home. "It's been such a sight of work."

"If you just take off the top rows, I could step out," suggested the prisoner. "Then leave the stones, and you two can step down into the prison tomorrow."

"Maybe we could let the Simpson twins be the prisoners. We could pretend they steal things like their father does."

"They needn't steal just because their father does," argued Rebecca. "Don't you ever talk about it in front of them if you want to be my friends. My mother tells me never to say hard things about people's own folks to their face. She says nobody can bear it, and it's wicked to shame them for what isn't their fault."

# CHAPTER FIVE

# A *Pink Dress* and a *Dark Storm*

Fall came, and Rebecca settled back into school. Friday afternoons were her favorite. This was the time for plays, songs, and reciting poetry. Most of the students disliked all this. But Rebecca brought a new spirit into these afternoons. She taught Elijah and Elisha Simpson to recite funny poems, which delighted everyone. She found a poem with very few "S's" for Susan, who talked with a lisp.

Rebecca and Emma Jane had a short play ready for a certain Friday afternoon. Miss Dearborn said it was *so* good she had invited the doctor's wife, the minister's wife, two members of the school committee, and a few mothers to the program.

The teacher asked Living Perkins and Rebecca to decorate the blackboards. Living drew the map of North America. Rebecca chose to do an American flag in red, white, and blue chalk.

The students gave a round of cheers for the blackboards. At this, Rebecca's heart leaped for joy. She felt tears rising in her eyes, and could hardly see the way back to her seat. In her lonely little life she had never received applause. This was a wonderful, dazzling moment.

The students became wildly excited about the program and began fixing up the room. Huldah Meserve covered the largest holes in the plastered walls with pretty branches. The water pail was filled with wild flowers. Minnie Smallie covered the ugly stove with wild ferns.

Miss Dearborn let the children go to lunch early. Those who lived near enough could go home to change clothes. Emma Jane and Rebecca excitedly ran nearly every step of the way.

"Will your Aunt Miranda let you wear your best, or only your brown dress?" asked Emma Jane.

"I think I'll ask Aunt Jane," Rebecca replied. "Oh! If my pink was only finished! Aunt Jane was to make the trim and finish the buttonholes!"

Rebecca found the side door locked, but she knew the key was under the step. (So did everyone else in Riverboro.) She unlocked the door and went in to find her lunch on the table. A note from Aunt Jane said they had gone to the next town to shop. Rebecca swallowed a piece of bread and butter, and flew up the front stairs to her room. On the bed lay the pink gingham dress, finished by Aunt Jane's kind hands. Could she—dare she— wear it without asking? Wouldn't they want her to look her best for the important visitors?

"I'll wear it," she decided. "It's only gingham after all. It's *only* grand because it's new. Well… and it does have trimming on it. And it *is* pink."

She unbraided her pigtails and tied her hair back with a ribbon. She changed her shoes, then slipped on the pretty frock. Downstairs, she glanced in the parlor mirror and was delighted. She danced out the side door, and covered the mile between the brick house and school in an *incredibly* short time.

"Rebecca Randall!" exclaimed Emma Jane at the school door. "You're pretty as a picture!'

"I?" laughed Rebecca. "Nonsense! It's only the pink gingham."

"How on earth did you get your Aunt Miranda to let you put on your brand new dress?"

"They were both away," Rebecca responded. "I thought she might have said yes."

The afternoon was perfect. All the students did well. There were no failures, no tears, and every parent was proud. Not one child forgot a word of the verses.

Rebecca was ready and willing and never shy. Wherever she stood was the center of the stage. Her clear high voice soared above all the rest in the choruses. Everybody watched her and began to feel some of her eagerness. She didn't try to take all the glory for herself, but brought the other children into the fun.

As she walked home after school, it seemed to Rebecca that she could never be cool and calm again. There were thick clouds gathering in the sky, but she took no notice of them. Fears could not live in the joy that flooded her soul. She was walking on air—until she entered the side yard of the brick house. There was Aunt Miranda standing in the open doorway. With a rush, Rebecca came back to earth.

"Rebecca, I want to talk to you. What did you put on that good new dress for, on a school day, without permission?"

"I would have asked if you were at home," began Rebecca.

"You knew that I wouldn't have let you."

"If I'd been *certain* you wouldn't have let me I'd never have done it," said Rebecca. "But I wasn't *certain*. I thought perhaps you might, if you knew that the minister's wife and the doctor's wife and the school committee would all be at school. I haven't hurt my dress a mite, Aunt Miranda."

"It's the sneakiness of your actions that's the worst," said Miranda coldly. "And look at the other things you've done! You went up the front stairs! You didn't even hide your tracks, for you dropped your hankie on the way up. You left the screen out of your bedroom window for the flies to come in. You never cleared away your lunch and you left the side door unlocked. Why, *anyone* coulda come in and stolen what they liked!"

Rebecca sat down heavily in her chair as she heard the list of her crimes. How could she have been so careless? The tears began to flow now as she tried to explain.

"Oh, I'm so sorry!" she faltered. "I was decorating the schoolroom, and it got late, and I ran all the way home. It was hard getting into my dress alone, and I hadn't time to eat but a mouthful. And just at the last minute, when I honestly—*honestly*—would have thought about clearing away and locking up, I looked at the clock and knew I could hardly get back to school on time."

"Don't wail and carry on now. It's no good cryin' over spilt milk," answered Miranda. "An ounce of good behavior is worth a pound of regret. Instead of tryin' to see how little trouble you can make in a house that ain't your own home, it seems as if you tried to see how much you could put us out. Now you step upstairs, put on your nightgown, go to bed, and stay there till tomorrow mornin'. You'll find a bowl of crackers and milk on your bureau, and I don't want to hear a sound from you till breakfast time. Jane, run and take the dishtowels off the line and shut the shed doors. We're goin' to have a turrible storm."

"I think we've already *had* the storm," said Jane quietly.

Rebecca closed the door of her bedroom. With trembling fingers, she took off the beloved pink gingham. She dabbed her wet eyes to keep the tears off the lovely dress that she had worn at such a price. She smoothed it out carefully, pinched up the white ruffle at the neck, and laid it away with an extra little sob.

All the while a resolve was growing in her mind to leave the brick house and let Hannah come to Riverboro in her place.

She had thought Aunt Miranda might be pleased that she had done so well at school. But there was no hope of pleasing her in any way.

Rebecca decided she would go to Cousin Ann's in Maplewood on the stagecoach the next day with Mr. Cobb. She would slip away now and see if she could stay all night with the Cobbs and be off next morning before breakfast.

With Rebecca, to think was to act. She put on her oldest dress and hat and jacket. Then she wrapped her nightdress, comb, and toothbrush in a bundle and dropped it softly out of the window. She scrambled out of the window, caught hold of the lightning rod, jumped to the porch, used the ivy trellis for a ladder, and was soon flying up the road in the storm.

# CHAPTER SIX

## A Rainbow Bridge

Jeremiah Cobb sat at his lonely supper at the table by the kitchen window. "Mother" (as he called his wife) was nursing a sick neighbor. Mrs. Cobb was mother only to a little headstone in the churchyard, where their little Sarah Ann was buried. The loss of their only child gave them a special love for all children.

The rain still fell, and the heavens were dark. Looking up from his tea, the old man saw at the open door the very picture of misery. It was Rebecca, but he hardly recognized her. Her face was swollen with tears.

"Please, may I come in, Mr. Cobb?" she said.

His big heart went out to her. "Why, you're soakin' wet. I made a fire, hot as it was, thinkin' I wanted somethin' warm for my supper. There, we'll hang your soppy hat on the nail, an' put your jacket over the chair. An' then you turn your back to the stove an' dry yourself good."

"Oh, Mr. Cobb," Rebecca cried, "I've run away from the brick house. I want to go back to the farm. Will you keep me tonight and take me up to Maplewood in the stage? I haven't got any money for my fare, but I'll earn it somehow afterwards."

"Well, I guess we won't quarrel 'bout money, you and me," said the old man. "Come over here aside of me an' tell me all about it. Jest set down on that there wooden stool an' out with the whole story to Uncle Jerry."

Rebecca leaned her aching head against the patched, comforting knee and told her story. It was a tragic story for this young girl, but she told it truthfully.

Uncle Jerry stirred in his chair a good deal, muttering, "Poor little soul!"

"You will take me to Maplewood, won't you, Mr. Cobb?" begged Rebecca.

"Don't you fret a mite," he answered slowly. "Now draw up to the table and take a bite o' somethin' to eat, child. How'd you like to set in Mother's place an' pour me out another cup o' hot tea?"

Rebecca smiled faintly, and dried her eyes.

Mr. Cobb went on. "I suppose your mother will be turrible glad to see you back again?"

A tiny fear in the bottom of Rebecca's heart stirred and grew larger.

"She won't like it that I ran away, I s'pose. And she'll be right sorry that I couldn't please Aunt Miranda."

"I s'pose she was thinkin' o' your schoolin', lettin' you come down here. But land! You can go to school in Temperance, I s'pose?"

"Temperance only has two months of school."

"Oh, well! There's other things in the world beside edjercation," responded Uncle Jerry.

"Ye-es, though Mother thought that was going to be the making of me," returned Rebecca sadly.

"How is this school down here in Riverboro—pretty good?" inquired Uncle Jerry.

"Oh, it's a splendid school! And Miss Dearborn is a splendid teacher!"

"You like her, do you? Well, Mother was talkin' to her this afternoon. 'How does the girl from Temperance git along?' asks Mother. 'Oh, she's the best scholar I have!' says Miss Dearborn."

"Oh, Mr. Cobb, *did* she say that?" whispered Rebecca. "I've tried hard all the time, but I'll study the covers right off of the books now."

"You mean you would if you were to stay here," said Uncle Jerry. "Now ain't it too bad you've got to give it all up on account o' your Aunt Mirandy? Well, I can't hardly blame ya. She's cranky an' she's sour. An' I guess you ain't much on patience, are ya?"

"Not very much," replied Rebecca.

"I'm not sayin' you were in the wrong. But if you were to do over again... I'd say... Well, your Aunt Mirandy gives you clothes and food and schoolin'. And she *is* goin' to send you to the Academy in Wareham at a big expense. She's turrible hard to get along with... And she does kinda throw reminders at ya 'bout how she's helpin' ya. Throws 'em like bricks, I'd say. But she is helpin' ya just the same. Maybe it's *your* job to kinda pay for 'em in good behavior. Jane's a leetle bit more easy goin' than Mirandy, ain't she?"

"Oh, Aunt Jane and I get along splendidly," exclaimed Rebecca. "I like her better all the time. She likes me, too. And she understands."

"Jane will be real sorry to find you've gone away, I guess. But never mind. It can't be helped. She'll have a dull time with Mirandy—without your company. Mother declares she's never seen Jane look so young 'n' happy."

There was a silence in the little kitchen, except for the ticking of the tall clock and the beating of Rebecca's heart. The rain stopped, and a sudden rosy light filled the room. Outside the window, a rainbow arch spanned the heavens like a bridge.

"The shower's over," said the old man. "It's cleared the air. It's washed the face o' the earth nice an' clean. Everything tomorrow will shine like a new pin—when you an' I are drivin' upriver."

Rebecca rose from the table, and put on her hat and jacket. "I'm not going to drive upriver, Mr. Cobb," she said. "I'm going to stay here and—catch bricks. I don't know if Aunt Mirandy will take me in after I've run away, but I'm going back now while I have the courage. Would you be so good as to go with me, Mr. Cobb?"

"You'd better b'lieve your Uncle Jerry will," said the old man delightedly. "Now you've had all you can stand tonight, poor little soul. Mirandy will be sore an' cross, so I've got a plan. I'll drive you over to the brick house in my buggy. I'll git out an' git your Aunt Mirandy 'n' Aunt Jane out into the shed to plan for a load o' wood I'm sendin' them. You'll slip out and go upstairs to bed. You see, you ain't run away yet. You've only come over here to *talk* to me 'bout runnin' away. An' we've decided it ain't worth the trouble, right? Not much wrong in all that, is there, now?"

And so, they carried out Uncle Jerry's plan, and Rebecca sneaked in and went upstairs.

As she slipped into bed, she was aching and throbbing in every nerve. Even so, she felt a kind of peace stealing over her and she went to sleep.

"I've never seen a child improve in her work as Rebecca has today," remarked Miranda Sawyer to Jane on Saturday evening. "She *is* the beatin'est child! That settin' down I gave her was probably just what she needed. And I daresay it'll last for a month."

"I'm glad you're pleased," returned Jane. "But I think you want a cringing worm, not a bright, smiling child. When Rebecca came downstairs this morning it seemed to me she'd grown old in the night. If you'll let her go to the County Fair in Milltown with the Cobbs on Wednesday, that'll hearten her up a little."

Rebecca and Emma Jane *did* go to the Fair. And it was impossible for two children to see more, do more, and talk more than those two happy girls.

# CHAPTER SEVEN

## *Rebecca's Punishment*

Rebecca got on in the brick house as best she could that autumn. She stayed out of trouble, and therefore suffered no punishments. However, one event—one sad accident—actually made her decide she ought to punish herself.

Wearing her best dress, Rebecca had gone to take tea with the Cobbs. While crossing the bridge, she was taken by the beauty of the river. She leaned over the rail to enjoy the dashing waterfall beneath. Resting her elbows on the topmost board, she stood there dreaming.

What she did not know was that the bridge had just been painted.

The waterfall was a swirling wonder of water at any time of the year. It sparkled in summer sunshine. It shone cold and gray in November. It swelled and roared in April. Rebecca never went across the bridge without stopping to take in the beauty. And at this moment she was trying to write a poem—when she suddenly became aware of the wet paint.

"Oh! It's all over my best dress! Oh, what *will* Aunt Miranda say! Surely Mrs. Cobb can help me!" And she flew up the hill crying.

Mrs. Cobb calmly said she was able to remove almost any stain from almost any fabric. She dressed Rebecca in one of her blue robes. While they ate the evening meal, she dipped the dress in paint thinner.

When supper was cleared away, Rebecca washed the dishes. Mrs. Cobb worked on the dress, and Uncle Jerry offered advice from time to time. At length they left the dress to dry, and went into the sitting room.

Mrs. Cobb sat by her mending basket, and Uncle Jerry took down a gingham bag of snarled strings to unravel. Rebecca busied herself writing out the poem she had been working on.

When she had finished, Rebecca read her poem aloud. Oh, the praises! The Cobbs thought it was beautiful. Maybe even better than Mr. Longfellow's famous poems!

After a while they went into the kitchen to check on the dress. It was quite dry, and looked a little better—but the colors had run into streaks! Mrs. Cobb smoothed it with a warm iron. Rebecca put it on to see if the smudges showed.

They did.

Rebecca gave one look and sighed a deep sigh. "Well, goodnight. If I've got to have a scolding, I want it quick, and get it over," she said bravely. Then she left to go face Aunt Miranda.

"Poor little unlucky thing!" said Uncle Jerry. "I know she gets dreamy and all… but I vow, if she was ours, I'd let her slop paint all over the house before I could scold her."

Rebecca took her scolding like a soldier—and there *was* a lot of it. Aunt Miranda told her she would have to wear her dress, stained as it was, until it was worn out. Aunt Jane, who felt sorry for the child, promised to make her an apron to hide the streaks.

After Rebecca went to her room, she began to think of a way to punish herself. She must give up something, she decided. But, truth be told, she had very little to give. As she sat by the window, she looked about the room. There was hardly anything but the beloved pink parasol. Her eyes moved from the parasol… to outside the window… and down to the water well. That would do. She would fling her "dearest thing in life" into the depths of the water!

As usual, she took action right away. She stole out the front door, lifted the cover of the well, gave one sad shudder, and flung the little pink treasure down.

Rebecca felt refreshed the next morning. She had punished herself, and her little soul was uplifted. With a happy heart, she went to school.

Meanwhile, Miss Miranda tried to pump water from the well after breakfast—with no luck. She called in Mr. Flagg for help. He lifted the cover, explored a bit, and found the problem. An ivory "hook" had caught in the chain gear—a little parasol handle… Not only that, he had to clear out a bent and twisted pink parasol that had *somehow* opened and jammed in the well.

When Rebecca tried to explain why she had thrown her beloved pink parasol into Miranda Sawyer's well, she indeed sounded ridiculous—even to her own ears. How *could* she explain to a person who closed her lips into a thin line and looked at her out of blank eyes?

"Now see here, Rebecca," said Aunt Miranda. "When you think you ain't punished enough, just tell me. I'll come up with something more. Whatever it is, it'll be something that won't punish the whole family, and make 'em drink ivory dust, wood chips, and pink silk rags with their water."

# CHAPTER EIGHT

## *Mr. Aladdin*

Just before Thanksgiving, the poor Simpson home was in despair. There was little to eat, and less to wear. Many kind-hearted villagers brought food and clothes. But life was rather dull and dreary in the chill and gloom of November. The Simpson children knew that other people would soon have feasts of turkey, and golden pumpkin pies, and delicious stuffing.

They needed something to take their minds off all this. A pamphlet from the Excelsior Soap Company caught their attention. If they sold bars of soap, door to door, they could earn prizes! And so this is what they set upon doing.

They sold enough soap bars to earn a child's handcart. And the pamphlet had pictures of bigger and better prizes! Oh, how they wanted the beautiful brass banquet lamp with a lovely paper shade! But to earn such a lamp, they would have to sell soap to every village around! The problem was that only the oldest, Clara Belle, was any sort of a saleslady. So they talked to Rebecca and Emma Jane, and the girls promised to help.

On a Saturday, the girls drove the Perkins' old white horse to North Riverboro, three miles away. They put several boxes of soap into the back of the wagon to sell. It was a glorious Indian summer day, a rustly day, a scarlet and tan, yellow and bronze day. The air was like sparkling cider, and every field had its heaps of yellow and brown harvest, all ready for the barns or markets. The old horse sniffed the sweet bright air, and trotted like a colt.

At each house the girls took turns. One would hold the horse. The other took the soap samples to the housewife.

They had not sold much soap by the time they drew up to one gateway with a very large house set back off the road.

"It's your turn, Rebecca," said Emma Jane.

Rebecca walked toward the house with her head held high. On the porch she saw a good-looking young man sitting in a rocking chair. He had an air of the city about him. He had a well-shaven face, well-trimmed mustache, and well-fitting clothes. Rebecca felt shy, but she asked, "Is the lady of the house at home?"

"I am the lady of the house at present," said the stranger, with a smile. "What can I do for you?"

"Have you ever heard of the—I mean I would like to introduce to you a very remarkable soap. It is called Rose Red and Snow White. For bathing and washing clothes."

"Oh! I know that soap," said the gentleman. "Made out of pure vegetable fats, isn't it?"

"The very purest," agreed Rebecca.

"And yet a child could do the wash with it."

Rebecca felt lucky to find a customer who knew all good things about the soap already. She eagerly sat down on a stool at his side near the edge of the porch. Before long, she forgot all about Emma Jane! She was talking as if she had known the young man all her life.

"I'm just on a visit to my aunt," explained the delightful gentleman. "I used to stay here as a boy, and I love the spot."

"I don't think anything takes the place of one's childhood farm," said Rebecca quite seriously.

"So you think your childhood is a thing of the past, do you, young lady?"

"I can still remember it," answered Rebecca, "though it seems a long time ago."

"I can remember mine well enough, and an unpleasant one it was," said the stranger.

"So was mine," sighed Rebecca. "What was your worst trouble?"

"Too little food and clothes, mostly."

"Oh!" exclaimed Rebecca. "Mine was no shoes and too many babies and not enough books. But you're all right and happy now, aren't you?" She thought to herself that he *looked* handsome and successful. Yet she could see that his eyes were sad when he was not speaking.

"I'm doing pretty well, thank you. Now tell me, how much soap should I buy today?"

"How much would your aunt need?"

"Oh, I don't know. Soap keeps, doesn't it?"

"I'm not certain, but I think so."

"What are you going to do with the great profits you get from this business?" he asked.

Rebecca found herself describing the Simpson family, and their desperate need of a banquet lamp to brighten their lives.

"How many more do they need to sell?"

"If they sell two hundred more cakes this month and next, they can have the lamp by Christmas," Rebecca answered. "And a hundred more to get the lampshade by summer time."

"I see. Well, that's all right. I'll take three hundred cakes. That will give them shade and all."

At this remark, Rebecca tipped over and tumbled into a clump of lilac bushes!

The amused young man picked her up, set her on her feet, and brushed her off.

"You should never seem surprised when you have taken a large order," he said. "You ought to have replied 'Can't you make it three hundred and fifty?' instead of tipping over in that unbusinesslike way."

"But it doesn't seem right for you to buy so much. Are you sure you can afford it?"

"If I can't, I'll save on something else." He smiled. "What is your name, young lady?"

"Rebecca Rowena Randall, sir."

"Do you want to hear my name?"

"I think I know already," answered Rebecca, with a bright glance. "I'm sure you must be Mr. Aladdin in *The Arabian Nights*—with the magic lamp that grants wishes! Oh, I must run down and tell Emma Jane."

Mr. Aladdin followed Rebecca to the wagon and took the soap.

"If you could keep a secret, it would be a nice surprise to have the lamp arrive at the Simpsons' on Thanksgiving Day, wouldn't it?" he asked.

They gladly agreed, and thanked him over and over. Tears of joy stood in Rebecca's eyes.

"Oh, don't mention it!" laughed Mr. Aladdin. "I like to see a thing well done. Good-bye, Miss Rebecca Rowena! Just let me know whenever you have anything to sell. I'm certain I shall want to buy it."

# CHAPTER NINE

## The Banquet Lamp

There was company at the brick house for Thanksgiving dinner. The Burnham sisters, from North Riverboro, had spent the holiday with the Sawyer sisters for the past twenty-five years.

Rebecca sat silent with a book after the dishes were washed. When it was nearly five she asked if she could go to the Simpsons'.

"The Simpsons have a new lamp!" said Rebecca. "The children got it as a prize for selling soap. And Emma Jane and I promised to go see it lighted and make it a kind of party."

"Well, you can go for a while, I s'pose," sniffed Aunt Miranda. "Seein' as it's Thanksgiving."

After she left, the Burnham sisters said that Rebecca had improved greatly since coming to the brick house.

"There's plenty of room left for improvement," answered Miranda. "Land, she's into everything! Gone to see a lamp! I didn't think those *Simpson* children had brains enough to sell anything."

"One of them must have," said Ellen Burnham. "The girl that was selling soap at the Ladds' home in North Riverboro—well now, Adam Ladd said she was the most remarkable child he ever saw."

"It must have been Clara Belle. And I would never call her remarkable," answered Miss Miranda. "Has Adam been home again?"

"Yes, he's been staying a few days with his aunt. There's no limit to the money he's making, they say. And to think we can remember the time he was a barefoot boy without two shirts to his name! It is strange he hasn't married, with all his money. And him so fond of children! He always has a pack of them at his heels."

"There's hope for him still, though," said Miss Jane. "He's just a young man."

"He could get a wife in Riverboro if he was a hundred and thirty," remarked Miss Miranda.

"Adam's aunt says he was so taken with the girl that sold the soap that he declared he was going to bring her a Christmas present," Miss Ellen went on. "He remarked about this child's handsome eyes. He said it was her eyes that made him buy the three hundred cakes."

The conversation made Jane nervous. What child in Riverboro could be described as remarkable and winning, *except Rebecca*? What child had wonderful eyes, *except Rebecca*? And finally, was there ever a child in the world who could make a man buy soap by the hundred cakes, *except Rebecca*?

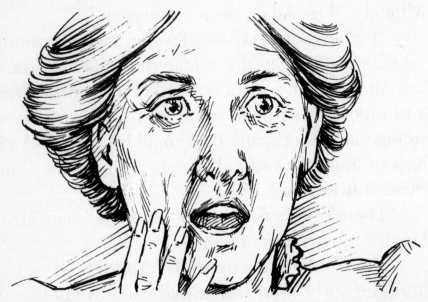

Meantime, the "remarkable" child had flown up the road in the deepening dusk. In a moment she was met by Emma Jane.

"I have a handful of nuts and raisins and some apples," said Rebecca.

"I have peppermints and maple sugar," said Emma Jane. "And the doctor gave them sweet potatoes and cranberries and turnips! Father sent a roast. And Mrs. Cobb gave them a chicken and a jar of mincemeat!"

At five-thirty, the Simpson house was a festive scene! The lamp itself seemed to be having the party and receiving the guests. The children had taken the one small table in the house and placed it in the far corner of the room. And on it stood the magical lamp!

Mrs. Simpson put the fire out. The lamp was lit. The brass glistened like gold. The red paper shade glowed like a giant ruby. The lamp flung a wide splash of light upon the floor. And in that soft light sat all the Simpson children in awe and solemn silence. Emma Jane and Rebecca stood behind them, hand in hand. No one spoke. The scene was too thrilling and serious for that.

When it was time for Rebecca and Emma Jane to go, Clara Belle said, "I'm so glad you both live where you can see it shine from our windows. I wonder how long it will burn without bein' filled? We don't have much kerosene."

"Oh, yes, we do!" cried Seesaw Simpson. "There's a great barrel of it settin' out in the shed! Mr. Tubbs brought it and said somebody sent an order by mail for it."

Rebecca squeezed Emma Jane's arm. "It must have been Mr. Aladdin," she whispered.

Rebecca entered the brick house dining room joyously. The Burnham sisters had gone and the two aunts were knitting.

"It was a heavenly party," she cried, taking off her hat and cape.

"Go back and see if you have shut the door tight, and then lock it," said Miss Miranda.

"And the lamp is lovely," said Rebecca, coming in again. "Aunt Jane, Aunt Miranda! Come into the kitchen and look out of the sink window. You can see it shining all red!"

Aunt Jane followed Rebecca into the kitchen.

"Rebecca, who was it that sold the three hundred cakes of soap to Mr. Ladd?"

"Mr. *Who?*" exclaimed Rebecca.

"Adam Ladd."

"Is *that* his real name? I didn't make a bad guess. Aladdin sounds like Adam Ladd, doesn't it!" Rebecca laughed softly to herself.

"Answer me, Rebecca."

"Oh! Emma Jane and I sold it. He needed the soap as a present for his aunt."

"I really wish you wouldn't do anything out of the ordinary without asking Mirandy first. You do such very odd things."

"There can't be anything wrong this time," Rebecca answered confidently. "Ever since we sold the soap, I have felt as if the banquet lamp was inside of me, all lighted up."

Rebecca's eyes were brilliant, and her cheeks were rosy. Her loose hair lightly tumbled in waves over her forehead.

"That's just the way you look, Rebecca—for all the world as if you *did* have a lamp burning inside of you," sighed Aunt Jane. "Rebecca! Rebecca! I wish you could take things easier, child. I am fearful for you sometimes."

On Christmas Day, Rebecca had exchanged gifts with her aunts when a knock came on the door. She was handed a package with her name on it. She took it like one in a dream and carried it into the dining room.

"It's a present. It must be," she said, looking at it in a dazed sort of way. "But I can't think who it could be from."

"A good way to find out would be to open it," remarked Miss Miranda.

Rebecca opened it with trembling fingers. Inside a pretty case was a long chain of pink coral beads with a cross made of coral rosebuds. A card with "Merry Christmas from Mr. Aladdin" lay under the cross. A silver chain with a blue locket was marked for Emma Jane. The card read:

*Dear Miss Rebecca Rowena,*

*I hope I have chosen the right gifts for you and your friend. You must wear your chain this afternoon, please, for I am coming over in my new sleigh to take you both for a drive. My aunt is delighted with the soap.*

*Sincerely, your friend,*

*Adam Ladd*

"Well, well!" cried Miss Jane. "Isn't that kind of him? Now eat your breakfast, Rebecca. After we've washed up the dishes you can run on over to Emma's and take her chain. What's the matter, child?"

Rebecca's joy was too deep for words. Tears filled her eyes and slowly fell down her cheeks.

Adam Ladd called as he promised, and met the two aunts. Rebecca wore her lovely pink coral necklace, and happiness and excitement filled her soul. The sleigh ride was the crowning moment of that glorious Christmas Day. Rebecca went to sleep many nights afterward with the precious coral chain under her pillow—with one hand on it to be certain that it was safe.

# CHAPTER TEN

## *Seasons of Change*

The next year or two brought growth and change for Rebecca. She did well in school and, for the most part, kept out of trouble. As Rebecca grew, her friends did also. Some left Riverboro. Dick Carter, Living Perkins, and Huldah Meserve enrolled in the Academy in Wareham. The Simpsons moved away. Rebecca and Emma Jane remained the best of friends. Yet, still, there was an emptiness inside her. She longed for a special friend who would understand what she felt in her heart. Emma Jane was dear, but she did not enjoy poetry and did not feel the rushes of joy that Rebecca could feel.

"Uncle Jerry" and "Aunt Sarah" Cobb were good friends. The sight of old Uncle Jerry always made Rebecca's heart warm. She often helped the old man dig potatoes or shell beans. And she sometimes stayed with him while he did his evening milking. He was the only person to whom she poured out her whole heart. He would listen to her hopes and dreams.

At the brick house, Rebecca practiced her scales and exercises on the old piano. But at the Cobbs' cabinet organ she sang like a bird. Here she was happy and loved. Still, she longed for somebody who not only loved but also understood her. Perhaps in the big world of Wareham there would be people who thought and dreamed and wondered as she did.

Rebecca shot up like a young tree. Aunt Jane could no longer let down her hems, and Aunt Miranda had to agree that new dresses were needed. Rebecca's old dresses were sent to Sunnybrook Farm to be made over for Jenny.

News came every month from Sunnybrook Farm. Rebecca's favorite brother, John, had his heart set on becoming a country doctor. Cousin Ann's husband had died, and John had gone to live with her. He was to have good schooling and the use of the old doctor's medical library. In return, he would care for the horse and cow and barn. There was a rumor that the new railroad might go near Sunnybrook Farm, and the land would rise in value. This was good news!

But there was sad news, too. Little Mira, the youngest child, had died. Rebecca went home for a sorrowful two-week visit. There she wept over a little grave under a willow tree at Sunnybrook Farm. Her mother was sad. The house was sad. All the years of penny-pinching and being poor seemed to add to the sadness. Especially for Rebecca, who was so sensitive to life and beauty.

Rebecca walked through all her familiar, secret places. There was the spot where the Indian pipes grew. The marshy ground where the flowers were largest and bluest. The maple tree where she found the oriole's nest. The hedge where the field mice lived. The moss-covered stump where the white toadstools sprang up as if by magic. And the hole at the root of the tall pine where an old toad made his home. These were the landmarks of her childhood, and she looked at them as across an endless distance.

Even the dear little brook was sad. In summer the merry stream had danced over white pebbles on its way to deep pools where it could be still and think. Now, like Mira, it was cold and quiet, wrapped in its shroud of snow. Rebecca knelt and put her ear to the glaze of ice. She imagined she could hear a faint, tinkling sound. It was all right! Sunnybrook would sing again in the spring. Perhaps Mira, too, would have her singing time somewhere.

# CHAPTER ELEVEN

## Rebecca Represents the Family

Rebecca was in her last year in the Riverboro school. She was thirteen and looking forward to going to the Academy in Wareham the next fall. She and Emma Jane, and other Riverboro schoolmates, would take the train to the bustling town—just like grown adults!

In March, Rebecca had a chance to show her aunts that the "wild little gypsy" was growing into a young lady. The church had a meeting for the visit of the Reverend Amos Burch and his family. They were missionaries returning from Syria. Both Miranda and Jane had taken bad colds, so Miranda sent Rebecca to represent the family.

At the church, Rebecca was asked to play the organ. Like a little adult, she agreed. Then Mr. Burch gave an inspiring talk on the work they were doing in Syria. It was so fascinating that many asked if he could talk more about how the people in Syria lived. Mr. Burch said he would the next evening—that is, if someone would let his family stay overnight.

There was a long, embarrassing silence.

Mrs. Robinson leaned over to Rebecca. "Your grandfather *always* entertained the missionaries when he was alive," she whispered.

She meant this for a stab at Miss Miranda, who did not like company. But Rebecca thought it was a suggestion. If it had been a former custom, perhaps her aunts would want her to do the right thing. And she *was* representing the family. Rebecca stood up straight and tall and invited the family to the brick house.

At home, Aunt Miranda was upset. "Explain, if you can, who gave you the right to invite strangers to stay here overnight? You know we ain't had any company for twenty years. And I don't intend to have any for another twenty—or at any rate while I'm the head of the house."

"Don't blame her, Miranda, till you've heard her story," said Jane.

Nervously, Rebecca explained. "Mrs. Robinson whispered to me that the missionaries *always* used to go to the brick house when grandfather was alive. So I thought I ought to invite them, since you weren't there to do it for yourself. Mr. Burch prayed for Grandfather, and called him a man of God, and thanked our Heavenly Father that his spirit was still alive in his daughters (that was you). And he was so glad that the good old brick house— where so many *other* preachers and missionaries had been helped—was still open for the stranger and traveler."

A gate in Miranda's heart swung open a little on its stiff and rusty hinges. Memories came to her of the old days and her beloved father.

"Well, I see you did the right thing, Rebecca," she said quietly.

"Now, since you're both sick, couldn't you trust me just once to get ready?" Rebecca asked.

"I believe I will," sighed Miranda. "I'll lay down and see if I can get strength to cook supper. It's half past three—don't you let me lay a minute past five, Rebecca."

Rebecca dashed upstairs like a whirlwind. The aunts could hear her scurrying to and fro, fluffing pillows and feather beds, flapping towels, and singing while she worked.

When she called her aunts at five o'clock, everything was ready. The missionary family arrived promptly, and Rebecca took over the care of their two little girls. There was a fine supper and a pleasant evening with members of the church who came in. The Burches told strange and beautiful stories about Syria. The two children sang, while Rebecca played the old piano for them.

At eight, Rebecca said, in her most grown-up voice, "Time for *little* missionaries to go upstairs!" The children said goodnight, and Rebecca took them up to bed.

Rebecca woke up before six the next morning, and quickly put on a robe and slippers. She stole quietly down the "forbidden" front stairs. Carefully, she closed the kitchen door behind her so that no noise would waken the rest of the household. She busied herself for a half-hour, getting breakfast ready. Then she went back to her room to dress before calling the children.

When Miranda and Jane opened the kitchen door, they stared in wonder. Had they strayed into the wrong house by mistake?

There was a roaring fire in the stove. The teakettle was singing and bubbling. A rich, welcoming scent came from the coffeepot. The potatoes and corned beef were on the wooden tray. The brown and white loaves were out. The toast rack was ready, the milk was skimmed, and the butter had been brought from the dairy.

Miranda and Jane exchanged glances.

"Ain't she the beatin'est child that ever was born into the world!" exclaimed Miranda. "But she can work when she's got a mind to! I declare she's all Sawyer!"

The day and the evening went by pleasantly. The Burches left with lively hearts and many thanks. Afterward, Miranda's feelings toward "the beatin'est child" were softer, though she didn't show them.

Later in life, Rebecca would look back on this visit with the Burches with pride. It was the first time she was asked to represent the family. She had done it well—and she had done it with love. It was a turning point in her life.

Have you ever noticed how gracious and mannerly you feel when you wear a beautiful new dress? Or how quiet and serious you feel when you close your eyes, clasp your hands, and bow your head? Or how good you feel when you listen politely to another person? Then you know how your actions—and how you stand and look—can change how you feel on the inside. And you know how Rebecca felt. She had *acted* grown up, so she *became* grown up.

# CHAPTER TWELVE

## *School in Wareham*

The day finally came! Rebecca and Emma Jane enrolled at Wareham Academy. They went on the train every day September to Christmas. Then they boarded in a rooming house in Wareham during the three coldest months. Aunt Miranda agreed to pay this expense.

Wareham was different from Riverboro—as different as Riverboro had been from Sunnybrook Farm. It was a pretty village with a broad main street shaded by great maples and elms. It had a drugstore, a blacksmith, a plumber, several shops and churches, and many boardinghouses. Life in the village centered on the Academy.

High school lasted four years, but Rebecca planned to finish in three years. She wanted to begin earning a living by the time she was seventeen. That way, she could help send her younger brothers and sisters to school. Emma Jane was not a good student, and could have stayed in Riverboro to finish. But she wanted to stay with Rebecca, so her parents agreed to let her go. Loyalty, after all, is as valuable in this world as brains and talent.

Rebecca studied English literature and writing with her favorite teacher, Miss Emily Maxwell. One day, Miss Maxwell asked each new student to bring her an essay written at their old school. Rebecca stayed after class and came shyly up to Miss Maxwell's desk.

"Miss Maxwell, I can bring you an old essay, but they were all bad. I never did like the topics we had to write about. I can't bear to show them. May I bring my poetry instead?"

Miss Maxwell agreed to look at the poetry. Rebecca left copies with her, and Miss Maxwell took them home to read, along with essays from the other students. A few days afterward she asked Rebecca to stay after class.

The room was quiet. Red leaves rustled in the breeze and flew in at the open window. Miss Maxwell sat by Rebecca's side on the bench.

"Did you think these were good?" she asked.

"Not so very," confessed Rebecca, "but it's hard to tell all by yourself."

Miss Maxwell decided that Rebecca would prefer the truth. "Well," she said smiling, "you were right. Your poetry needs some work."

"Then I must give up all hope of ever being a writer!" sighed Rebecca. "Must I never try any more poetry?"

"You have a natural sense of rhyme and meter, Rebecca. You should keep trying. When you are older, I think you may write very good verses. Poetry needs knowledge and vision, experience and imagination, Rebecca. You have a great deal of imagination and vision and the rest will come. You'll enjoy the first essay. I'm going to ask all the new students to write a letter to their family telling of their town and school life."

"Do I have to write it as *myself*?" asked Rebecca.

"What do you mean?"

"Well, you see, if I write a letter from Rebecca Randall to her sister Hannah at Sunnybrook Farm the letter would have to be rather dull. But now, if I could make believe I was a *different* girl, and could write to someone who could understand everything I said, I could make it nicer."

"I think that's a delightful plan," said Miss Maxwell. "And whom will you pretend to be?"

"A noble, rich girl with golden hair! She has come to live in Wareham where her father lived when he was a boy, long before he made his fortune. The father is dead now, and she has a guardian, the best and kindest man in the world. He is sometimes very quiet and serious, but sometimes happy and full of fun. I shall call her Evelyn! And her guardian's name shall be Mr. Adam Ladd."

"Do you *know* Mr. Ladd?" asked Miss Maxwell in surprise.

"Yes, he's my very best friend," cried Rebecca delightedly. "Do you know him, too?"

"Oh, yes. He is a trustee of this school, you know. He often comes here. I'm sure he will enjoy a letter from 'Evelyn' if I may show it to him."

Rebecca said yes.

Miss Maxwell soon reported to Adam Ladd that she had found a pearl in his young friend. Adam agreed heartily.

# CHAPTER THIRTEEN

## *A Heart in Bloom*

"How d'ye *do*, girls?" chirped Huldah Meserve. She peeped into Rebecca and Emma Jane's room one Friday. "Oh, *do* stop studying a minute and show me your room! It's simply too cute for words! I don't know what gives it that simply *gorgeous* look. Is it Rebecca's lamp? Or that elegant screen? You certainly do have it looking good."

"Isn't this your study hour?" Rebecca asked. She was a little upset at being bothered.

"Yes, but I *had* to go downtown for some gloves. And then I went to the principal's office to see if my Latin grammar book that I lost had been handed in. That's the reason I'm dressed *so* fine."

Huldah was stylish and she flirted with any boy who was near. Today she was wearing a sporty blue woolen dress with a gray jacket. Her gray felt hat had a white tissue veil with large black dots. It made her delicate skin look brilliant. Her open jacket showed several society pins to prove how popular she was.

"There was a perfectly elegant gentleman in the principal's office," Huldah went on, dancing into the room. "He was a stranger to me. He was handsome as a picture and had on a stylish suit of clothes. His only jewelry was a cameo scarf pin and a perfectly *gorgeous* ring—it wound round and round his finger. Oh dear, I must run! There's the class bell!"

A ring that wound round the finger? Rebecca knew that ring. Mr. Aladdin wore one like it. Her *own* Mr. Aladdin, who was so kind and generous to her. Every Christmas he gave her and Emma Jane a special gift. He had called several times at the brick house to say hello to her aunts. Sometimes he wrote from Boston and asked her the news of Riverboro. She would send him pages of gossip. If Huldah's "stranger" turned out to be Mr. Aladdin, would he come to see her?

On Fridays, Rebecca always spent a few hours at Miss Maxwell's home before she caught the train to Riverboro. And so today she ran down the path through the pine woods to the large white house on a quiet village street. The maid knew to take her to Miss Maxwell's library room. She could wait there for Miss Maxwell to come from class for a half-hour of talk.

She selected *David Copperfield* and sank into a seat by the window. When she had read for half an hour, she glanced out of the window. Whom should she see but Huldah coming from the path through the woods *with Mr. Aladdin!* Huldah was holding her skirts daintily. She was stepping lightly in her very grown-up high-heeled shoes. Her cheeks were glowing, and her eyes were sparkling under the black and white veil.

Rebecca slipped from her seat by the window to the rug before the bright fire. She leaned her head on the seat of the great easy chair. There was a strange storm in her heart, and it frightened her. She never minded that Emma Jane was part of her friendship with Mr. Aladdin. Yet she could not bear to give up any part of that friendship to *Huldah*.

Suddenly the door opened quietly. "Miss Maxwell told me I should find Miss Rebecca Randall here."

Rebecca was startled by the sound and sprang to her feet. "Mr. Aladdin!" she said joyfully. "Oh! I knew you were in Wareham, and I was afraid you wouldn't have time to see me."

"But I will always make time for you, Rebecca."

The light in the room grew softer, the fire crackled cheerily. They talked of many things, for they had not seen each other for months. Rebecca asked him how he came to be a trustee of the Wareham Academy.

"My mother used to be a trustee of the school. Several years after she died, I accepted the position in her memory. Her last happy years were spent here. She was married a month after she graduated, and she lived only until I was ten. Would you like to see my mother, Rebecca?"

He handed Rebecca a leather case. She took it gently and opened it. Inside was an innocent, pink-and-white daisy of a face that went straight to the heart.

"Oh, what a sweet, sweet, flowery face!" she whispered softly.

"The bitter weather of the world bent the flower and dragged it to the earth. She died for lack of love and care. I was only a child and could do nothing to protect her. All that I have gained in life seems, now and then, so useless—since I cannot share it with her!"

Rebecca was seeing a new Mr. Aladdin. Her heart gave a throb of understanding and sympathy. This explained the tired look in his eyes, under the laughter.

"I'm so glad I know," she said, "and so glad I could see her just as she was then. I wish she could have been kept happy, and had lived to see you grow up strong and good. She would have been so proud to know how you turned out. But... perhaps she *does* know."

"You are a comforting little person, Rebecca," said Adam, rising from his chair.

Rebecca rose, too. Small tears were trembling on her lashes. The young man looked at her suddenly as if with new eyes.

"Why, little Rose Red-Snow White is making way for a new girl!" he said. He took her slim brown hands in his. "I believe you are becoming a young lady!"

"Oh, Mr. Aladdin!" cried Rebecca "I am not fifteen yet. It will be three years before I'm a young lady of seventeen!"

"Rebecca," he said, after a moment's pause, "who is that young girl with a lot of pretty red hair and very fancy manners? She walked with me down the hill. Do you know whom I mean?"

"It is Huldah Meserve."

Adam put a finger under Rebecca's chin and looked into her clear eyes.

"Don't form yourself on her, Rebecca," he said seriously. "Clover blossoms that grow in the fields beside Sunnybrook must not be tied in the same bouquet with showy sunflowers. They are too sweet and fragrant and wholesome."

# CHAPTER FOURTEEN

## Aladdin Grants Some Wishes

Rebecca studied all during her summer vacation. On her return in the autumn, she passed special exams. This would allow her to finish in two more years. She wasn't a remarkable scholar, but her bright, imaginative answers delighted her teachers.

By the spring of the second year, she had become a leader at the school—just as she had been in Riverboro. She was elected assistant editor of the Wareham Academy newspaper. She was the first girl to have that position.

"She'll always get votes," said Huldah Meserve. "I only wish *I* was tall and dark-haired and had the gift of making people believe I could do great things, like Rebecca Randall. There's one thing though. The boys call her pretty, but you notice they don't really give her much attention."

Rebecca *was* pretty. The boys *did* notice her. But Rebecca just did not have much interest in boys—even for fifteen and a half!

Rebecca's studies kept her very busy. She still had to worry about the difficult problems of daily living. *And* she was very concerned about matters at the brick house and at the farm.

During the autumn and winter of that year, Rebecca felt as if Aunt Miranda was even more grumpy and picky. She seemed to find fault with Rebecca at every turn.

One Saturday, Rebecca had run upstairs to Aunt Jane and burst into a flood of tears. "Aunt Jane," she exclaimed, "sometimes I think I can't stand Aunt Miranda's constant scolding. Nothing I can do suits her."

Aunt Jane cried with Rebecca as she tried to soothe her. "You must be patient," she said. She wiped away Rebecca's tears, and then her own. "I haven't told you, for I didn't want to trouble you when you're studying so hard… but your Aunt Miranda isn't well. One Monday morning about a month ago, she had what the doctor thought was a little stroke. She's failing right along, and that's what makes her so fretful."

Rebecca stopped crying. "Oh, the poor dear thing! I won't mind a bit what she says now. Perhaps it won't be as bad as you think."

Things were not well at Sunnybrook Farm, either. The time for paying the interest on the mortgage had come and gone. For the first time in fourteen years, they did not have the forty-eight dollars to pay the bank.

The only happy news from Sunnybrook Farm was Hannah's engagement to marry Will Melville. He was a young farmer with land right next to Sunnybrook. Hannah was blissful and excited. However, she was *so* happy, she never gave a thought to her own mother's worries. And she gave no thought to earning any money to help pay on the mortgage.

One cold spring day, Adam Ladd was driving through the Boston streets. In a shop window he saw a rose-colored parasol. It reminded him of Rebecca. She had once told him about *another* little pink parasol that had met a tragic end. He bought the parasol and sent it to Wareham at once. Then, an hour later he realized he had not thought of Emma Jane! He returned quickly to buy a blue parasol.

He sometimes went to Temperance now on business. There was a new railroad being built, and he was on the planning board. Every land owner hoped the tracks would go through *their* land, for the railroad would pay quite a bit of money for the land. There was a chance that the tracks would go through Sunnybrook Farm. If they did, Mrs. Randall would be well paid.

Adam Ladd came to Wareham one day straight from Temperance. While he was there, he had a long walk and talk with Rebecca. He noticed that she was looking pale and thin.

She wore her long black braids wrapped about her head. Her front hair framed her face in loose waves. Adam looked at her in a way that made her put her hands over her face and laugh through them shyly.

"I know what you are thinking, Mr. Aladdin," she said. "That my dress is an inch longer than last year, and my hair different. But I'm not nearly a young lady yet. Sixteen is a month off still."

He only responded by saying that perhaps she was studying too hard. But after a little more talk, he realized why she looked so tired. She was worried about the overdue payment on the farm.

After their talk, Adam went to the principal's office. He told the principal that he wanted to sponsor an essay contest for the older students. He would give cash prizes. To himself he thought: *If Rebecca could win—and she is a fine writer—she could pay the debt on the farm.*

Then Adam visited Miss Maxwell.

"Miss Maxwell, doesn't it strike you that our friend Rebecca looks awfully tired?"

"She does indeed," agreed Miss Maxwell. "And I plan to take her with me to my favorite retreat, at spring vacation."

"What a wonderful idea. But, let me help with her traveling costs. I can only give her such help through you. I am greatly interested in Rebecca, and have been for some years."

"Oh, but don't pretend *you* discovered her," said Miss Maxwell warmly, "for I did that myself."

"She was a dear friend of mine long before she came to Wareham," laughed Adam. "Are you planning to take Emma Jane also?"

"No. I prefer to have Rebecca all to myself."

"I can understand that," he said, without thinking. "I mean, of course!" he added hastily. "One person is easier to travel with than two."

Here they saw Rebecca walking down the quiet street with a lad of sixteen. They were reading something aloud to each other. Their heads were bent close together over a sheet of paper. Rebecca kept glancing up at the boy, her eyes sparkling.

"I don't think that I believe boys and girls should be in the same school!" Adam said, looking unhappy.

Miss Maxwell smiled at his jealousy, and added quickly, "You are watching the senior and the junior editors of the school newspaper, *The Pilot*, walking together!"

# CHAPTER FIFTEEN

## *The Gates of Childhood*

The vacation with Miss Maxwell was more than Rebecca could imagine! She had her first glimpse of the ocean. The strange new scenes and the freedom thrilled her. She had always hungered for new things to see and learn. She loved life and thirsted for beauty. She had a great need for the music and the poetry of life! Now life had grown all at once rich and sweet, wide and full.

Miss Maxwell told her of the essay contest, and this stayed on her mind. Oh! She could never be happy unless she won it. How proud Mr. Aladdin would be! She came back from her vacation with many new ideas and thoughts for it.

The summer term ended and graduation was held for Huldah Meserve, Dick Carter, Living Perkins, and the other seniors. At graduation the essay winners were announced. Huldah received second prize. But the first prize went to Rebecca, who wasn't even a senior yet! She immediately took the money to her mother at Sunnybrook Farm to pay the mortgage interest.

Hannah had married Will already. So Rebecca stayed for a while to help her mother adjust to managing the farm without Hannah.

Back at school, her last year seemed to go by like a fast train, and graduation day soon dawned. Rebecca stole softly out of bed, crept to the window, threw open the blinds, and welcomed the rosy light. Somehow, even the sun looked different on this special day—larger, redder, more important than usual.

Parents and relatives of the seniors had been coming on the train and driving into town since breakfast time. Lines of buggies and wagons were drawn up along the sides of the shady roads. The streets were filled with people wearing their best clothes. The female seniors were seated in their bedrooms, while mothers hovered over them.

The mothers combed and fussed and fixed hair ribbons. Then the girls slipped on the prettiest dotted or white Swiss muslin dresses. Rebecca couldn't afford Swiss muslin. She and Emma Jane had dresses of plain white muslin trimmed with fine hand stitching.

The two girls waited in their room alone. Emma Jane was rather tearful, for this was the last day they would be together. Rebecca had been offered two positions, and surely she would choose one and move away. One position was as a piano teacher at a girl's boarding school in Augusta. The other was an assistant's place in the Edgewood High School. The pay was not much for either position. Rebecca liked the music teacher job, for she could practice her music while she taught.

Rebecca grew more excited as the day went on. When the first bell rang through the halls, she took in a breath. In five minutes the class would line up for graduation! She stood at the window, speechless, with her hand on her heart.

"It is coming, Emmie. We are closing the gates of childhood behind us. I can almost see them swing. I can almost hear them clang. And I can't tell whether I am glad or sorry."

"I don't care how they swing or clang," said Emma Jane, "as long as we're are on the same side of the gate. But we won't be. I know we won't!"

"Emmie, don't you dare cry! For I'm just on the brink myself! If only you were graduating with me. That's my only sorrow. Hug me once for luck, dear Emmie."

Ten minutes later, Adam Ladd came into the main street and stopped to watch the graduates stride down the road to the meeting house. He stood under the elms in the old village street where his mother had walked so many years before. He was just turning toward the church when he heard a little sob. Behind a hedge in the garden was a forlorn person in white.

He stepped inside the gate and said, "What's wrong, Miss Emma?"

"Oh, is it you, Mr. Ladd? Rebecca wouldn't let me cry, but I must. I'm not graduating with Rebecca! Not that I mind that. I just can't stand being separated from Becky!"

The two walked together along the street and into the church, while Adam tried to comfort the sad girl. Rebecca waved and smiled when she saw them sitting together.

Rebecca also saw Hannah and Will with John and Cousin Ann. She felt a pang that her mother could not leave the farm, even for this day. But she smiled again when she saw the Cobbs. No one could fail to see Uncle Jerry. He was so thrilled and didn't even try to hide his tears. He had told *every* neighbor about the marvelous graduate whom he had known ever since she was a child.

There were other Riverboro faces, but where was Aunt Jane? Rebecca knew that Aunt Miranda could not come, but where, on this day of days, was her beloved Aunt Jane? However, this thought came and went in a flash as the day's events began. She played the piano, she sang, she recited the prayer like one in a dream.

And then... it was over! The diplomas were presented with a wild round of applause for each graduate. After the crowd had thinned a little, Adam Ladd made his way to the platform.

Rebecca met him in the aisle. "Oh, Mr. Aladdin, I am so glad you could come! Tell me"— and she looked at him half shyly—"tell me, Mr. Aladdin—did I do all right?"

"More than all right!" he said warmly. "I'm glad I met the girl. I'm proud I know the young lady."

Adam left the church and came upon Miss Maxwell. They always *did* seem to end up talking about Rebecca, and this day was no different.

"I believe that happier days are dawning for her," said Adam. "You must keep this a secret, but Mrs. Randall's farm will be bought by the new railroad. She will receive six thousand dollars. That's not a fortune, but she'll make three to four hundred dollars a year, if she will let me invest it for her."

"Then Rebecca won't be burdened with debt on the farm," said Miss Maxwell softly. "That is as it should be. For she has talent. She has a future. And she must follow her destiny."

"Yes, she must," said Adam.

"Mmm. Especially if the destiny follows your own, yes?" Miss Maxwell smiled.

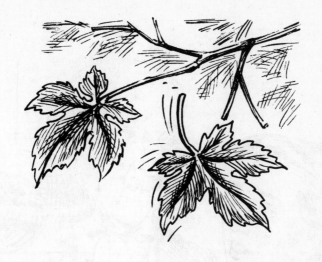

# CHAPTER SIXTEEN

## *Leaving Childhood Behind*

Rebecca had barely told Adam Ladd good-bye when Mr. and Mrs. Cobb came to her side.

"Where—where is Aunt Jane?" she cried.

"I'm sorry, lovey, but we've got bad news."

"Is Aunt Miranda worse? She is! I can see it by your looks." Rebecca's color faded.

"She had a second stroke yesterday morning jest when she was helpin' Jane lay out her things to come here today. Jane said you wasn't to know anything about it till graduation was all over."

"I will go right home with you, Aunt Sarah. Poor Aunt Miranda! And I've been so happy all day, except that I missed Mother and Aunt Jane."

"There ain't no harm in bein' happy, lovey. That's what Jane wanted you to be."

"I'll pack your trunk for you, Becky," said Emma Jane. She had come toward them and heard the sad news.

They moved into one of the quiet side pews, where Hannah and Will and John joined them. Classmates called out to Rebecca: "Don't be late for the picnic lunch!" and "Come early to the class party tonight!" But all the excitement became a blur to her. Nothing seemed real.

Aunt Miranda's mind was perfectly clear when Rebecca got to the brick house. She could not move, however. Her pale, sharp face, framed in its nightcap, looked so tired on the pillow. Her body was so very still under the blanket.

"Let me look at you," said the old aunt in her cracked, weak voice. "I hope you won't neglect things in the kitchen because I ain't there. Do you still clean out the coffeepot and turn it upside down on the windowsill?"

"Yes, Aunt Miranda."

"It's always 'yes' with you, and 'yes' with Jane," groaned Miranda. "But I lay here knowin' there's things done the way I don't like 'em."

Rebecca sat down by the bedside and timidly touched her aunt's hand. Her heart swelled with tender pity at the thin face and closed eyes.

"You're not to worry about anything. Here I am all grown up and graduated. Look at me, big and strong and young, all ready to go into the world and show what you and Aunt Jane have done for me. I've had two good positions offered to me already. If you want me near, I'll take the Edgewood school. That way I can be here nights and Sundays to help. When you get better, then I'll go to Augusta. That's a hundred dollars more, with music lessons and other things beside."

"You listen to me," said Miranda in a shaky voice. "Take the best place, regardless of my sickness. I'd like to live long enough to know you'd paid off that mortgage, but I guess I won't."

Here the old woman stopped. This was the most she had talked in weeks. Rebecca went out of the room, to cry by herself.

The days went on, and Miranda grew stronger. Before long she could be moved into a chair by the window. Little by little, hope stole back into Rebecca's young heart. She began to get her clothes ready to go to Augusta.

At length the day dawned when her trunk was packed. Then, when all was ready, a telegram came from Hannah:

COME AT ONCE.
MOTHER HAS HAD A BAD ACCIDENT.

In less than an hour, Rebecca was on her way to Sunnybrook Farm instead of Augusta. There she found that her mother's right knee was broken and her back was strained from a fall. She was in no danger, but she had to stay in bed.

Rebecca wrote the news to her aunts. After they read the letter, Miranda gathered the strength to talk.

"There's things I want to go over with you, Jane. Don't tell Rebecca. I've willed her the brick house. But now, mind you, I *do* plan to take my time 'bout dyin'. And I don't want to be thanked, neither. I s'pose she'll use the front stairs as instead of the back stairs… but, well, maybe when I've been dead a few years I won't let that bother me. She'll want you to stay and have your home here as long as you live. But anyway, I've wrote it down that way."

Jane knit silently as she looked at the poor, sad figure lying weakly on the pillows. She only stopped knitting from time to time to wipe the tears from her own eyes.

Two months went by for Rebecca at Sunnybrook Farm. It was two months of steady, tiring work and weary nights of watching by her mother's bedside.

Rebecca thought of those splendid visions she had during graduation! How fleeting they were. Now her life was filled with dull daily duty. Then one day she received a letter from the school in Augusta. The music position had been filled. Her spirit sagged. Her heart ached. She felt like it was beating against the door of a cage. She longed for the freedom of the big world outside.

But there were moments of joy during those gray days of daily living. As she stirred a cake, or kneaded bread dough, her imagination still wandered. And as she listened to the kitchen fire crackling, and the teakettle whistling, she found herself singing. Her heart had not lost its wings.

The bare little farmhouse *was* dreary, but the children's love for her was comforting. And mother and daughter began to know each other in a new way—as two grown women.

One mellow October morning, Rebecca came into her mother's room with her arms full of autumn leaves. It was a marvelous morning. The air was fragrant with ripening fruit. There was a funny little bird on a tree outside the door nearly bursting his throat with joy of living. He had forgotten that summer was over, and winter was coming. Aurelia heard the bird and looked at her tall, splendid daughter.

Then suddenly she covered her eyes and cried, "I can't bear it! Here I lie chained to this bed, keeping you from everything you want to do. It's all wasted! All my saving and doing without. All your hard study. All Mirandy's money goin' for school and clothes. Everything that we thought was going to be the making of you!"

"Mother, Mother, don't talk so, don't think so!" exclaimed Rebecca. "Why, Mother, I'm only a little past seventeen! The old maple by the well that's a hundred years old had new leaves this summer—so there must be hope for me!"

"I only hope you won't have to wait too long for your leaves, Rebecca," she said. "Your life looks very hard and rough to me. Your Aunt Miranda is a cripple at the brick house. You're taking care of me here at the farm. You've had to work hand and foot, nursing first your aunt and then me."

"I suppose there *ought* to be fears in my heart," Rebecca said. She walked to the window and looked out at the trees. "But there aren't. Something stronger sweeps them out— something like a wind. Oh, Mother! There is Hannah's husband, Will, driving up the lane. He ought to have a letter from the brick house."

# CHAPTER SEVENTEEN

## *"Good-bye, Sunnybrook"*

Will Melville drove up to the window. He tossed a letter into Rebecca's lap, then went off to the barn on an errand.

Rebecca opened the envelope. In one flash of an eye she read the whole brief page.

*Your Aunt Miranda passed away an hour ago. Come at once, if your mother is out of danger. I shall not have the funeral till you are here. She died very suddenly and without any pain.*

*Oh, Rebecca! I long for you so!*

*—Aunt Jane*

Rebecca burst into a passion of tears. "Poor, poor Aunt Miranda! She is gone without ever really being happy in life. And I couldn't say good-bye to her! Poor lonely Aunt Jane! What can I do, Mother? I feel torn in two, between you and the brick house."

"You must go this very instant," said Aurelia, raising herself from her pillows. "Your aunts have done everything in the world for you. It is your turn to pay back some of their kindness and show your gratitude. Jenny can take care of the house somehow, if Hannah will come over once a day.

"Oh, how I wish I could go to my sister's funeral. I'd like to tell her that I've forgotten and forgiven all she said when I was married. Her acts were softer than her words.

"I remember so well when we were little girls together. She took such pride in curling my hair. Another time, when we were grown up, she let me wear her best blue muslin dress. It was when Lorenzo—before he was your father!—had asked me to lead the grand march with him at the Christmas dance. And I found out afterward that Miranda thought he would ask her! And still, she lent me her dress."

There was only an hour to pack. Will Melville would drive Rebecca to Temperance. A neighbor lady would sleep at the farm in case Mrs. Randall needed any help in the night.

Rebecca flew down over the hill to get a last pail of spring water. As she lifted the bucket from the crystal brook, she looked out over the glowing beauty of the autumn landscape. She saw a group of men looking though some instruments of some kind. They were writing in notebooks, and had strung lines of rope between posts in the ground.

The lines crossed Sunnybrook at her favorite spot where the pond lay clear and still. Yellow leaves sat on its quiet surface. Its sand was sparkling in the sun. Rebecca knew at once what the men were doing. They were surveying land for the new railway.

She caught her breath.

*The time has come!* she thought. *I am saying good-bye to Sunnybrook. The gates that almost swung together that last day in Wareham will close forever, now. Good-bye, dear brook and hills and meadows. You are going to see life, too. We must be always hopeful that the best is yet to be.*

Will had seen the surveyors, too. At the post office, he heard how much Mrs. Randall was sure to get for her land. He was very pleased! His land was next to hers, and it would be more valuable, now, also. In the buggy, he felt like whistling all the way to Temperance. But Rebecca's own sad face kept him quiet.

"Cheer up, Becky!" he said, as he left her at the station. "Your mother will be fine soon. And the next thing you know, your family will be moving to some nice little house close to wherever you work." Then he drove away to tell Hannah the good news.

Adam Ladd was waiting at the train station. He came up to Rebecca as she entered the door.

"I know you are sad this morning," he said, taking her hand.

She opened her heart and told him of her grief. He gave her his sympathy and asked if he might come soon to the brick house to see her.

He helped her on the train to Maplewood, and they said their good-byes. Adam thought that Rebecca was, in her sad dignity, more beautiful than he had ever seen her. She was a beautiful person—and a beautiful woman.

He turned from the little country station to walk in the woods until his own train would be leaving. There he threw himself under a tree to think and dream. He had brought a new copy of *The Arabian Nights* for Rebecca. He wanted to replace her well-worn old one. But he had forgotten to give it to her—after meeting at such a sad time.

He turned the pages slowly, and came to the story of "Aladdin and the Wonderful Lamp." The old tale held him spellbound, just as it had in the days when he first read it as a boy. But there was one part he found himself reading over and over. This was the part where Aladdin is filled with happiness because the princess admits that she loves him and wishes to marry him.

## *Aunt Miranda's Apology*

Rebecca got off the train at Maplewood and hurried to the stagecoach to Riverboro. She was overjoyed to see Uncle Jerry Cobb standing there next to the horses.

"My drivin' days are over," he explained, "but I came for you. So here I am, jest as I was more'n six year ago. Will ya sit up in front with me?" A warm smile spread across the old man's face.

Rebecca flung herself on Mr. Cobb's dusty shoulder, crying like a child.

"Oh, Uncle Jerry!" she sobbed. "It's all so long ago, and so much has happened. And so much is *going* to happen that I'm fairly frightened."

"There, there, lovey," the old man whispered. "We'll talk things over as we go along the road. Maybe things won't look so bad."

Every mile of the way was familiar. And all the time, Rebecca was thinking back to the day, so long ago, when she sat on the box seat for the first time. Her legs had dangled in the air, too short to reach the footboard. She could see the pink parasol, and feel the stiffness of the tan dress. The two friends drove along mostly in silence. But it was a sweet, comforting silence to both of them.

In Riverboro, she saw a white cloth fluttering from the Perkins' attic window. It was Emma Jane's loving "hello" to warm her heart until they could meet. Black scarves hung over the blinds of the brick house. The brass knocker was covered with a black cloth.

"Stop, Uncle Jerry! Don't turn in at the side. Let me run up the path by myself."

The door of the brick house opened just as Rebecca closed the gate behind her. Aunt Jane came down the stone steps, frail and white. Rebecca held out her arms. Then, warmth and strength and life flowed from the young lady into the older woman.

"Rebecca," she said, raising her head, "before you go in to look at her, do you feel any bitterness over anything she ever said to you?"

Rebecca's eyes blazed. She said in a choking voice, "Oh, Aunt Jane! I am going in with a heart full of gratitude!"

"She was a good woman, Rebecca. She had a quick temper and a sharp tongue, but she wanted to do right. And she did it as near as she could. She never said so, but I'm sure she was sorry for every hard word she spoke to you. She didn't take her words back in life. But she acted so that you'd know her feelings when she was gone."

"I told her before I left that she really had been the making of me," sobbed Rebecca.

"God made you in the first place. And I'd say you've done a lot yourself to help Him along," said Aunt Jane. "But she gave you the means to do it and that ain't to be looked down on. And she did give up some of her own luxuries to do it. Now let me tell you something, Rebecca. Your Aunt Mirandy has left all this to you in her will. The brick house and buildings. All the furniture. And the land all round the house."

Rebecca put her hand to her heart. After a moment's silence she said, "Let me go in alone. I want to talk to her. I want to thank her. I feel as if I could make her hear and feel and understand."

Jane went back into the kitchen. Even death does not stop daily duties. The table still must be laid, the dishes washed, and the beds made, by somebody.

Ten minutes later, Rebecca came outside from the parlor looking white and tired, but calm. She sat in the quiet doorway. Here she was shaded from the little Riverboro world by the overhanging elms. A wide sense of thankfulness and peace came over her as she looked at the autumn landscape. She listened to the rumble of a wagon on the bridge. She heard the call of the river as it dashed to the sea. She put up her hand softly and touched first the shining brass knocker and then the red bricks, glowing in the October sun.

It was home—her roof, her garden, her green acres, her dear trees. It was shelter for the little family at Sunnybrook. Her mother and Aunt Jane would once more be together. Her mother would be with old friends from her girlhood. The children would have teachers and playmates.

And she? Her own future was still folded and closed from view. It was folded and hidden in beautiful mists. She leaned her head against the sun-warmed door. She closed her eyes and whispered, just as if she had been a child saying her prayers:

"God bless Aunt Miranda. God bless the brick house that was. God bless the brick house that is to be!"

## THE END

## KATE DOUGLAS WIGGIN

Kate Douglas Smith was born in Philadelphia in 1856. Her father died when she was young, and her family moved to Maine. There, her mother remarried and they settled in the small town of Hollis. Much like Rebecca Randall, Kate received her education through home study, district school, a female seminary, and an academy. This was a lot of education for a girl of her times!

Kate began teaching kindergarten in 1877 and soon started Silver Street Kindergarten in San Francisco, the first kindergarten in California. She married Bradley Wiggin in 1881. As a married woman, she was not allowed to teach, but she still loved children. Her first books, including *The Birds' Christmas Carol*, were written to raise money for the Kindergarten.

When Kate's first husband died suddenly in 1889, she began writing more. In 1895 she married George Christopher Riggs, who strongly supported her writing. *Rebecca of Sunnybrook Farm*, Kate's most famous book, was written in 1903.

She died in Harrow, England, August 24, 1923, while attending a writing conference.